Dear Arjun

Enid Blyton's

THE MYSTERY
OF THE SPITEFUL LETTERS

i

First published in Great Britain 1946
by Methuen & Co. Ltd.
This edition first published 1990 by Dean
an imprint of the Hamlyn Publishing Group
Published 1996 by Mammoth
an imprint of Reed International Books Ltd,
Michelin House, 81 Fulham Road, London SW3 6RB
and Auckland, Melbourne, Singapore and Toronto

Reprinted 1997

ISBN 0 7497 1970 2

A CIP catalogue record for this book is available at the British Library

Enid Blyton's

THE MYSTERY

OF THE SPITEFUL LETTERS

MAMMOTH

CONTENTS

1   THE EXTRAORDINARY TELEGRAM

BETS and Pip were waiting impatiently for Larry, Daisy and Fatty to come. Bets was on the window-seat of the playroom looking anxiously out of the window.

'I wish they'd buck up,' she said. 'After all, they came home from boarding-school yesterday, and they've had plenty of time to come along. I do want to know if Fatty's got any more disguises and things.'

'I suppose you think there'll be another first-class mystery for us to solve these hols,' said Pip.

'Golly, that was a wizard one we had in the Christmas hols, wasn't it?'

'Yes,' said Bets. 'A bit too wizard. I wouldn't really mind not having a mystery these hols.'

'*Bets!* And I thought you were such a keen detective!' said Pip. 'Don't you want to be a Find-Outer any more ?'

'Of course I do. Don't be silly !' said Bets.

'I know you don't think I'm much use, because I'm the youngest and only nine, and you're all in your teens now— but I did help an awful lot last time, when we solved the mystery of the secret room.'

Pip was just about to say something squashing to his little sister when she gave a yell. 'Here they are ! At least—here are Larry and Daisy. Let's go down and meet them.'

They tore downstairs and out into the drive. Bets flung herself on the boy and girl in delight, and Pip stood by and grinned.

'Hallo, Larry ! Hallo, Daisy ! Seen Fatty at all ?'

'No,' said Larry. 'Isn't he here ? Blow ! Let's go to the gate and watch for him. Won't it be fun to see old Buster again too, wagging his tail and trotting along on his short Scottie legs!'

The four children went to the front gate and looked out. There was no sign of Fatty and Buster. The baker's cart drove by. Then came a woman on a bicycle. Then up the lane plodded a most familiar figure.

It was Mr. Goon the policeman, or old Clear-Orf as the children called him. He was going round on his beat, and was not at all pleased to see the four children at Pip's gate, watching him. Mr. Goon did not like the children, and they certainly did not like him. There had been three mysteries to solve in their village of Peterswood in the last year, and each time the children had solved them before Mr. Goon.

'Good morning,' said Larry politely, as Mr. Goon came by, panting a little for he was plump. His frog-eyes glared at them.

'So you're back again, like bad pennies,' he said. 'Ho ! Poking your noses into things again, I suppose!'

'I expect so,' said Pip cheerfully. Mr. Goon was just about to make another crushing remark when there came a wild ringing of bicycle bells and a boy came round the corner at top speed on a bicycle.

'Telegraph-boy,' said Pip. 'Look out, Mr. Goon, look out !'

The telegraph-boy had swerved right over to the police-man, and it looked as if he was going straight into him. Mr. Goon gave a yelp and skipped like a lamb out of the way.

'Now then, what you riding like that for ? A public danger, that's what you boys are !' exploded Mr. Goon.

'Sorry, sir, my bicycle sort of swerved over,' said the boy. 'Did I hurt you, sir ? I'm down-right sorry !'

Mr. Goon's temper cooled down at the boy's politeness. 'What house are you wanting ?' he asked.

'I've got a telegram for Master Philip Hilton,' said the telegraph-boy, looking at the name and address on the orange envelope in his hand.

'Oh ! Here's Pip !' said Bets. 'Oooh, Pip— a telegram for you !'

'The boy propped his bicycle by the side of the pavement, its pedal catching the kerb. Bur he didn't balance it very firmly and it fell over with a clatter, the handle-bar catching Mr. Goon on the shin.

He let out such a yell that all the children jumped. He hopped round, trying to hold his ankle and keep his balance too. Bets gave a sudden giggle.

'Oh, sir, I'm sorry !' cried the boy. 'That dratted bike ! It's always falling over. Don't you be angry with me, sir. Don't you report me, will you ? I'm that sorry !'

Mr. Goon's red face was redder than ever. He glared at the telegraph-boy, and rubbed his ankle again. 'You deliver your telegram and clear-orf,' he said. 'Wasting the time of the post-office, that's what you're doing !'

'Yes, sir,' said the boy meekly, and gave Pip the orange envelope. Pip tore it open, full of curiosity. He had never had a telegram sent to him before.

He read it out loud. It was from Fatty.

'SORRY NOT TO SEE YOU THESE HOLS. HAVE GOT A MYSTERY TO SOLVE IN TIPPY-LOOLOO, AND AM LEAVING BY AEROPLANE TO-DAY. ALL THE BEST ! FATTY.'

The children crowded round to see the telegram. They couldn't believe their ears. What an extraordinary telegram ! Mr. Goon could hardly believe his ears either.

'You let me see that,' he said, and took it out of Pip's hand. He read it out loud to himself.

'This is from that boy Frederick Trotteville, isn't it ?' he said. 'Fatty, you call him, don't you ? What does it mean ? Leaving by aeroplane for Tippy-Tippy-whatever it is. Never heard of the place in my life !'

'It's in South China,' said the telegraph-boy unexpectedly. 'I got an uncle out there, that's how I know.'

'But—but—why should Fatty go—why should he solve a mystery out there—why, why . . .' began the four children, absolutely taken aback.

'We shan't see him these hols,' suddenly wailed Bets, who was extremely fond of Fatty, and had looked forward very much to seeing him.

'And a good thing too,' said Mr. Goon, giving the telegram back to Pip. 'That's what I say. A jolly good thing too. He's a tiresome nuisance that boy is, pretending to play at being a detective—and using disguises to deceive the Law—and poking his nose in where it's not wanted. Perhaps we'll have a little peace these holidays if that interfering boy has gone to Tippy—Tippy—whatever it is.'

'Tippylooloo,' said the telegraph-boy, who seemed as much interested as any one else. 'I say, sir—is that telegram from that clever chap, Mr. Trotteville? I've heard about him.'

'*Mr.* Trotteville !' echoed Mr. Goon, indignantly. 'Why, he's no more than a kid. *Mr.* Trotteville ! Mr. Interfering Fatty, that's what *I* call him !'

Bets gave a sudden giggle again. Mr. Goon had gone purple. He always did when he was annoyed.

'Sorry, sir. Didn't mean to make you all hot and bothered, sir,' said the telegraph-boy, who seemed very good indeed at apologizing for everything. 'But of course we've all heard of that boy, sir. Very very clever chap, he seems to be. Didn't he get on to some big plot last hols, sir, before the police did ?'

Mr. Goon was not at all pleased to hear that Fatty's fame was apparently spread abroad like this. He did one of his snorts.

'You got better things to do at the post-office than listen to fairy-tales like that !' he said to the eager telegraph-boy. 'That boy Fatty's just an interfering little nuisance and always was, and he leads these kids here into trouble too. I reckon their parents'll be pretty glad that boy's gone to Tippy—Tippy—er...'

'Tippylooloo,' said the telegraph-boy obligingly. 'Fancy him being asked out there to solve a mystery, sir. Coo, he must be clever !'

The four children were delighted to hear all this. They knew how the policeman must hate it.

'You get along now,' said Mr. Goon, feeling that the tele-graph-boy was a real nuisance. 'Clear-orf ! You've wasted enough time.'

'Yes sir ; certainly, sir,' said the polite boy. 'Fancy that fellow going off to Tippylooloo—by aeroplane too. Coo ! I must write to my uncle out there and get him to tell me what Mr. Trotteville's doing. Coo !'

'Clear-orf !' said Mr. Goon. The boy winked at the oth-ers and took hold of his bicycle handles. The children couldn't help liking him. He had red hair, freckles all over his face, red eyebrows and a funny twisty mouth.

'He got on his bicycle, did a dangerous swerve towards Mr. Goon, and was off down the road ringing the two bells he had as loudly as ever he could.

'There's a boy that's civil and respectful to the Law,' said Mr. Goon to the others. 'And he's an example to follow, see !'

But the other children were no longer paying attention to the fat policeman. Instead they were looking at the telegram again. How surprising it was ! Fatty *was* surprising, of course—but to go off by plane to China !

'Mother would never let *me* do a thing like that,' said Pip. 'After all, Fatty's only thirteen. I can't believe it !'

Bets burst into tears. 'I did so want him to come back for the hols and find another mystery !' she wailed. 'I did, I did!'

'Shut up, Bets, and don't be a baby,' said Pip. 'We can solve mysteries without Fatty, can't we ?'

But privately each of them knew that without Fatty they

couldn't do much. Fatty was the real leader, the one who dared to do all kinds of things, the real brain of the Find-Outers.

'Without Fatty we're like rabbit-pie without any rabbit in it,' said Daisy dolefully. That sounded funny, but nobody laughed. They all knew what Daisy meant. Things weren't nearly so exciting and interesting without Fatty.

'I just can't get over it,' said Larry, walking up the drive with the others. 'Fatty off to South China! And what *can* be the mystery he's solving there ? I do think he might have found time to come and tell us.'

'That telegraph-boy thought an awful lot of Fatty, didn't he ?' said Bets. 'Fancy! Fatty must be getting quite famous!'

'Yes. Old Clear-Orf didn't like him praising up Fatty, did he !' chuckled Larry. 'I liked that boy. He sort of reminded me of some one, but I can't think who.'

'I say—what's going to happen to Buster?' suddenly said Bets, stopping still in the drive. 'Fatty wouldn't be allowed to take his dog with him—and Buster would break his heart left alone. What do you suppose is happening to him ? Couldn't *we* have him?'

'I bet Fatty would like us to have him,' said Pip. 'Let's go up to Fatty's house and ask his mother about Buster. Come on. We'll go now.'

They all turned and went back down the drive. Bets felt a little comforted. It would be some thing to have Fatty's dog, even if they couldn't have Fatty. Dear old Buster! He was such a darling, and had shared all their adventures.

They came to Fatty's house and went into the drive. Fatty's

mother was picking some daffodils for her vases, and she smiled at the children.

'Back for the holidays?' she said. 'Well, I hope you'll all have a nice time. You're looking very solemn. Is anything the matter?'

'Well—we just came to see if we could have Buster for the hols,' said Latty. 'Oh, there he is! Buster, Buster old fel-low ! Come here!'

2   FATTY REALLY IS SURPRISING

BUSTER came tearing up to the children, barking madly, his tail wagging nineteen to the dozen. He flung himself on them and tried to lick and bark at the same time.

'Good old Buster!' said Pip. 'I bet you'll miss Fatty!'

'It was a great surprise to hear that Fatty has gone to China,' said Daisy to Mrs. Trotteville. Fatty's mother looked surprised.

'In an aeroplane too!' said Larry. 'You'll miss him, won't you, Mrs. Trotteville?'

'What exactly do you mean?' asked Mrs. Trotteville, looking as if she thought the children had gone mad all of a sudden.

'Gracious—Fatty can't have told her!' said Bets, in a loud whisper.

'Told me *what*?' said Mrs. Trotteville, getting impatient. 'What's the mystery? What's Fatty been up to?'

'But—but—don't you know?' stammered Larry. 'He's

gone to Tippylooloo, and...'

'Tippylooloo! What's all this nonsense?' said Mrs. Trotteville. She raised her voice. 'Frederick! Come here a minute!'

The children turned breathlessly to the house —and out of the front door, stepping lazily, came Fatty! Yes, it really was Fatty, as large as life, grinning all over his plump face. Bets gave a loud shriek and ran to him. She hugged him.

'Oh, I thought you'd gone to Tippylooloo! Didn't you go? Oh, Fatty, I'm so glad you're here!'

The others stared. They were puzzled. 'Did you send us that telegram?' said Daisy suddenly. Was it a joke on your part, Fatty?'

'What telegram?' asked Fatty innocently. 'I was just about to come down and see you all.'

'This telegram!' said Pip, and pushed it into Fatty's hand. He read it and looked astonished.

'Somebody's been playing a joke on you,' he said. he said. 'Silly sort of joke. And anyway, fancy you all believing I was off to Tippylooloo! Gosh!'

'You and your jokes!' said Mrs. Trotteville. 'As if I should let Frederick go to China, or whatever that ridiculous Tippylooloo place is. Now, if you want to go and talk to Frederick, either go indoors or go for a walk.'

They went indoors. They still felt very puzzled. Buster danced round, barking in delight. He was overjoyed because the whole company of Find Outers was together again.

'Who delivered this telegram?' asked Fatty.

'The telegraph-boy,' said Pip. 'A red-haired chap with freckles and a cheeky kind of voice. He let his bike-handle catch old Clear-Orf on the shin ! You should have seen him dance round!'

'Hm,' said Fatty. 'There's something strange about that telegraph-boy, *I* think! Delivering a telegram I didn't send! Let's go out and look for him and ask him a few questions !'

They went out, and walked down the lane together, Buster at their heels. 'You go that way, Larry and Daisy, and you go the opposite way, Pip and Bets,' said Fatty. 'I'll take this third way. We'll scour the village properly for that boy, and meet at the corner by the church in half an hour's time.'

'I want to go with *you,* Fatty,' said Bets.

'No, you go with Pip,' said Fatty, unexpectedly hard-hearted. He usually let Bets have her own way in every-thing. Bets said nothing but walked off with Pip, feeling rather hurt.

Larry and Daisy saw no telegraph-boy at all, and were waiting by the church corner in twenty-five minutes' time. Then Pip and Bets came up. They hadn't seen him either. They looked up and down for Fatty and Buster.

Round the corner came a bicycle, and on it was—the red-headed telegraph-boy, whistling loudly. Larry gave a yell.

'Oy! Come over here a minute!'

The telegraph-boy wobbled over, and balanced himself by the kerb. His red hair fell in a big lock over his forehead, and his uniform cap was well on one side.

'What's up, mate?' he said.

'It's about that telegram,' said Larry. 'It's all nonsense! Our friend Frederick Trotteville hasn't gone to China—he's here!'

'Where?' said the boy, looking all round.

'I mean he's in the village somewhere,' said Larry. 'He'll be along in a minute.'

'Coo!' said the boy. 'I wouldn't half like to see him! He's a wonder, he is! I wonder the police don't take him on, and get him to help them with their problems.'

'Well, we *all* helped to solve the mysteries you know,' said Pip, beginning to feel that it was time he and the others got a bit of praise too.

'No, did you really?' said the boy. 'I thought it was Mr. Trotteville that was the brains of the party. Coo, I'd like to meet him! Do you think he'd give me his autograph?'

The children started at him, thinking that Fatty must indeed be famous if telegraph-boys wanted his autograph.

'That was a dud telegram you brought,' said Larry. 'A fake, a joke. Did *you* fake it?'

'Me fake it! Coo, I'd lose my job!' said the telegraph-boy. 'Look here, when's this famous friend of yours coming? I want to meet him, but I can't wait here all day. I've got to get back to the P.O.'

'Well, the post-office can wait a minute or two, I should think', said Pip, who felt that none of them had got very much information out of the telegraph-boy, and was hoping that perhaps Fatty might.

A small dog rounded the corner, and Bets gave a yell. 'Buster! come on, Buster! Where's Fatty? Tell him to hurry.'

Every one thought that Fatty would come round the corner too, but he didn't Buster trotted on towards them alone. He didn't growl at the telegraph-boy. He gave him a lick and then sat down beside him on the kerb, turning adoring eyes up to him.

Bets was most astonished. She had never seen Buster adoring any one but Fatty in that way. She stared at the little black dog, surprised. What should make him like the telegraph-boy so much?

Then she gave a loud squeal and pounced on the telegraph-boy so suddenly that he jumped.

'Fatty!' she said. 'Oh, Fatty! What idiots we are! FATTY!'

Pip's mouth fell open. Daisy stared as if she couldn't believe her eyes. Larry exploded and banged the telegraphy-boy on the back.

'You wretch! You absolute wretch! You took us all in properly—and you took old Clear-Orf in too. Fatty, you're a marvel. How do you do it?'

Fatty grinned at them all. He removed his red eyebrows with a pull. He rubbed off his freckles with a wetted hanky. He shifted his red wig a little so that the others could see his sleek black hair beneath.

'Fatty! It's the most wonderful disguise!' said Pip enviously. 'But how do you manage to twist up your mouth to make it different and screw up your eyes to make them smaller and all that kind of thing?'

'Oh, that's just good acting,' said Fatty, swelling a little with pride. 'I've told you before, haven't I, that I always take the chief part in our school plays, and this last term I...'

But the children didn't want to hear about Fatty's wonderful doings at school. They had heard about those too often. Larry interrupted him.

'Golly! Now I know why the telegraph-boy praised you up so! Idiot! Calling yourself *Mr.* Trotteville and waiting for your own autograph! Honestly, Fatty, you're the limit!'

They all went to Pip's house and were soon settled in the playroom, examining Fatty's cap and wig and everything.

'It's a new disguise I got,' explained Fatty. 'I wanted to try it out, of course. Fine wig, isn't it? It cost an awful lot of money. I daren't tell Mother. I could hardly wait to play that joke on you. I'm getting awfully good at disguises and acting.'

'You are, Fatty,' said Bets generously. 'I would never have known it was you if I hadn't noticed Buster sitting down looking up at you with that sort of adoring look he keeps for you, Fatty.'

'So that's how you guessed, you clever girl!' said Fatty. 'I call that pretty good, Bets. Honestly, I sometimes think you notice even more than the others!'

Bets glowed, but Pip did not look too pleased. He always thought of Bets as his baby sister, and thought she ought to be kept under, and not made conceited about herself.

'She'll get a swelled head,' he growled. 'Any of us could have spotted Buster's goofy look at you.'

'Ah, but you didn't, said Fatty. 'I say—isn't it great that old Clear-Orf thinks I've gone to Tippylooloo! That *was* a bit of luck, his happening to be with you when I cycled up this morning. Didn't he jump when I let my bike fall on his shin!'

They all stared at Fatty in admiration. The things he did! The things he thought of! Bets giggled.

'Won't he be surprised when you turn up!' she said. 'He'll think you've come back from Tippylooloo already!'

'What a name!' said Daisy. 'How in the world did you

think of it?'

'Oh, things like that are easy,' said Fatty modestly. 'Poor old Clear-Orf! He just swallowed that telegram whole!'

'Are you going to use that disguise when we solve our next mystery?' asked Bets, eagerly.

'What's our next mystery?' said Pip. 'We haven't got one! It would be too much to expect one these hols.'

'Well, you never know,' said Fatty. 'You simply never know! I bet a mystery will turn up again—and I jolly well hope we'll be on to it before old Clear-Orf is. Do you remember how I locked him up in the coal-hole in our last mystery?'

Every one laughed. They remembered how poor old Mr. Goon had staggered up out of the coal-hole, black with coal-dust, his helmet lost, and with a most terrible sneezing cold.

'And we sent him some carbolic soap and found his helmet for him,' remembered Daisy. 'And he wasn't a bit grateful, and never even thanked us. And Pip's mother said it was rather an insult to send him soap and was cross with us.'

'I'd like another mystery to solve,' said Pip. 'We'll all keep our ears and eyes open. The hols have begun well, with you in your new disguise, Fatty—taking old Goon in as well as us!'

'I must go,' said Fatty, getting up. 'I've got to slip back and change out of this telegraph-boy's suit. I'll just put on my wig and eyebrows again in case I meet Clear-Orf. Well—so long!'

3   OH, FOR A MYSTERY!

A WHOLE week went by. The weather was rather dull and rainy, and the children got tired of it. It wasn't much fun going for walks and getting soaked. On the other hand they could't stay indoors all day.

The five of them and Buster met at Pip's each day, because Pip had a fine big playroom. They made rather a noise sometimes, and then Mrs. Hilton would come in, looking cross.

'There's no need to behave as if you were a hurricane and an earthquake rolled into one!' she said, one day. Then she looked in surprise at Pip. 'Pip, what on earth are you doing?'

'Nothing, Mother,' said Pip, unwinding himself hurriedly from some weird purple garment. 'Just being a Roman emperor, that's all, and telling my slaves what I think of them.'

'Where did you get that purple thing,' asked his mother. 'Oh, *Pip*— surely you haven't taken Mrs. Moon's bed-spread to act about in?'

'Well, she's out,' said Pip. 'I didn't think it would matter, Mother.'

Mrs. Moon was the cook-housekeeper, and had been with the Hiltons only a few months. The last cook was in hospital ill. Mrs. Moon was a really wonderful cook, but she had a very bad temper. Mrs. Hilton was tired of hearing her grumble about the children.

'You just put that bed-spread back *at once!*' she said. 'Mrs. Moon will be most annoyed if she thinks you've been into

her bedroom and taken her bed-covering. That was wrong
of you, Pip. And will you all please remember to wipe your
feet when you come in at the garden-door this wet weather?
Mrs. Moon says she is always washing your muddy foot-
marks away.'

'She's a spiteful old tell-tale,' said Pip sulkily.

'I won't have you talking like that, Pip,' said Mrs. Hilton.
'She's a very good cook and does her work extremely well.
It's no wonder she complains when you make her so much
extra cleaning—and, by the way, she says things sometimes
disappear from the larder and she feels sure it's you children
taking them. I hope that's not so.'

Pip looked uncomfortable. "Well, Mother,' he began, 'it's
only that we're most awfully hungry sometimes, and you
see . . .'

'No, I don't see at all, said Mrs Hilton. 'Mrs. Moon is in
charge of the larder, and you are not to take things without
either my permission or hers. Now take back that bed-spread,
for goodness sake, and spread it out neatly. Daisy, go with
Pip and see that he puts it back properly.'

Daisy went off meekly with Pip. Mrs. Hilton could be
very strict, and all five children were in awe of her, and of
Mr. Hilton too. They would not stand any nonsense at all,
either from their own children or from other people's! Yet
they all liked Mrs. Hilton very much, and Pip and Bets
thought the world of her.

Daisy and Pip returned to the playroom. Mrs. Hilton had
gone. Pip looked at the others and grinned.

'We put it back.' he said. 'We pulled it this way and that,
we patted it down, we draped it just right, we . . .'

'Oh, shut up!' said Larry. 'I don't like Mrs. Moon. She may be a good cook—and I must say she makes marvellous cakes—but she's a tell-tale.'

'I bet poor old Gladys is scared of her,' said Daisy. Gladys was the housemaid, a timid, quite little thing, ready with shy smiles and very willing to do anything for the children.

'I like Mrs. Cockles the best,' said Bets. 'She's got a lovely name, I think. She's the char-woman. She comes to help Mrs. Moon and Gladys twice a week. She tells me all kinds of things.'

'Good old Cockles!' said Pip. 'She always hands us out some of Mrs. Moon's jam-tarts on baking day, if we slip down to the kitchen.'

Larry yawned and looked out of the window. 'This disgusting weather!' he said. 'Raining again! It's jolly boring. I wish to goodness we'd got something to do—a mystery to solve, for instance.'

'There doesn't seem to be a single thing,' said Daisy. 'No robberies—not even a bicycle stolen in the village. Nothing.'

'I bet old Clear-Orf will be pleased if we don't get a mystery this time,' said Fatty.

'Has he seen you yet?' asked Bets. Fatty shook his head.

'No. I expect he still thinks I'm away at Tippylooloo,' he said a grin. 'He'll be surprised when I turn up.'

'Let's go out, even if its *is* raining,' said Pip. 'Let's go and snoop about. Don't you remember how last hols I snooped round an empty house and found that secret room at the top of it? Well, let's go and snoop again. We might hit on *something*!'

So they all put on macks and sou'-westers and went for a snoop. 'we might find some clues,' said Bets hopefully.

'Clues to *what*!' said Pip scornfully. 'You have to have a mystery before you can find clues, silly!'

They snooped round a few empty houses, but there didn't seem anything extraordinary about them at all. They peered into an empty shed, and were scared almost out of their wits when a tall tramp rose up from the dark corners and yelled at them.

They tramped over a deserted allotment and examined a tumble-down cottage at one end very thoroughly. But there was absolutely nothing odd or strange or mysterious to find.

'It's tea-time,' said Fatty. 'We'd better go home. I've got an aunt coming. See you tomorrow!'

Larry and Daisy drifted off home too. Pip and Bets splashed their way down their wet lane and went gloomily indoors.

'Dull and boring!' said Pip, flinging his mack down on the hall-cupboard floor. 'Nothing but rain! Nothing to do!'

'You'll get into a row if you leave your wet mack on the ground,' said Bets, hanging hers up.

'Pick it up then,' said Pip, in a bad tamper. He hadn't even an exciting book to read. His mother had gone out to tea. He and Bets were alone in the house with Gladys.

'Let's ask Gladys to come up to the playroom and play cards,' said Pip. 'She loves a game. Mrs. Moon isn't in to say No.'

Gladys was only too delighted to come and play. She was about nineteen, a pretty, dark-haired girl, timid in her ways, and easily pleased. She enjoyed the game of Happy

Families as much as the two children did. She laughed at all their jokes, and they had a very happy time together.

'It's your bed-time now, Miss Bets,' she said at last. 'And I've got to go and see to the dinner. Do you want me to run your bath-water for you, Miss?'

'No, thank you. I like doing it myself,' said Bets. 'Goodbye, Gladys. I like you!'

Gladys went downstairs. Bets went to run the bath-water. Pip went off whistling to change into a clean suit. His parents would not let him sit up to dinner unless he was clean and tidy.

'Perhaps it will be fine and sunny to-morrow,' thought Pip, looking out of the window at the darkening western sky. 'It doesn't look so bad to-night. We might be able to get a few bike-rides and picnics in if only the weather clears.'

It *was* fine and sunny the next day. Larry, Daisy, Fatty and Buster arrived at Pip's early, full of a good plan.

'Let's take our lunch with us and go to Burnham Beeches,' said Larry. 'We'll have grand fun there. You should just see some of the beeches, Bets—enormous old giants all gnarled and knotted, and some of them really seem to have faces in their knotted old trunks!'

'Oooh—I'd like to go,' said Bets. 'I'm big enough to ride all the way with you this year. Mummy wouldn't let me last year.'

'What's up with your Gladys?' said Fatty, scratching Buster on the tummy, as he lay upside down by his chair.

'Gladys? Nothing!' said Pip. 'Why?'

'Well, she looked as if she'd been crying when I saw her in the hall this morning,' said Fatty. 'I came in at the garden door as usual, and bumped into her in the hall. Her eyes looked as red as anything.

'Well, she was quite all right last night,' said Pip, remembering the lively game they had had 'Perhaps, the got into a row with Mrs. Moon.'

'Shouldn't think so,' said Fatty. 'Mrs. Moon called out something to her quite friendly as I passed. Perhaps she's had bad news.'

Bets felt upset. She went to find Gladys. The girl was sweeping the bedroom floors. Yes, her eyes were very red!

'Gladys, have you been crying?' asked Bets. 'What's the matter? Has somebody been scolding you?'

'No,' said Gladys, trying to smile. 'Nothing's the matter, Miss Bets. I'm all right. Right as rain.'

Bets looked at her doubtfully. She didn't look at all happy. What could have happened between last night and now?

'Have you had bad news?' said Bets, looking very sympathetic.

'Now just you heed what I say,' said Gladys. 'There is nothing the matter. You run off to the others.'

There was nothing to do but go back. 'She *has* been crying,' said Bets, 'but she won't tell me why.'

'Well, leave her alone,' said Larry, who didn't like crying females. 'Why should we pry into her private affairs? Come on, let's go and ask about this picnic.'

Mrs. Hilton was only too glad to say that the children could go off for the day. It was tiring having them in the house all day long, especially as Pip's playroom was the general meeting-room.

'I was going to suggest that you went off for the day

myself,' she said. 'You can take your lunch *and* your tea, if you like! I'll get it ready for you, whilst Fatty and the others go back to get theirs.

It was soon ready. Mrs. Hilton gave them the packets of sandwiches and cake. 'Now just keep out for the whole day and don't come tearing back because you're bored,' she said firmly. I don't want to see any of you till after tea. I've got important things to do to-day.'

'What are they, Mother?' asked Pip, hoping he was not going to miss anything exciting.

'Never you mind,'said his mother. 'Now, off you go and have a lovely day!'

They rode off on their bicycles. 'Mother seemed to want to get rid of us to-day, didn't she?' said Pip. 'I mean—she almost *pushed* us out. I wonder why? And what's so important to-day? She didn't tell us about any Meeting or anything.'

'You're trying to make it out to be quite a mystery!' said Bets. 'I expect she's going to turn out cupboards or something. Mothers always seem to think things like that are very important. Hurrah, Pip—there are the others! Come on!'

With a jangling of bicycle bells the little party rode off. Buster sat solemnly in Fatty's basket. He loved a picnic. A picnic meant woods or fields, and woods or fields meant one thing and one thing only to Buster—rabbits!

THE children had a lovely day. It was warm and sunny, there were primroses everywhere, and the little bright mauve dog-voilets made a carpet with the wind-flowers.

'This is glorious,' said Daisy. 'Thank goodness the weather's changed at last. Let's lay out our macks and sit on them.'

Buster went off happily. The children watched him go. 'Off to solve the great Rabbit Mystery!' said Fatty. 'Where is the rabbit-hole that is big enough to take a dog like Buster's always hoping to solve.'

Every one laughed. 'I wish we had a great problem to solve,' said Daisy. 'I've sort of got used to having something for my brains to chew on each hols. It seems odd not to have anything really to think about.'

The day passed quickly. It was soon time to go home again, and the five mounted their bicycles. Buster had with difficulty been removed from halfway down a rather big rabbit-hole. He had been very angry at being hauled out, and now sat sulkily in Fatty's basket, his ears down. Just as he had almost reached that rabbit! Another minute and he'd have got him!

'Buster's sulking,' said Pip, and laughed. 'Oy, Buster! Cheer up!'

'I wonder if Mother's done all the important things she said she had to do,' said Bets to Pip. 'Anyway she can't say she's been much bothered with us to-day!'

They all parted at the church corner to go their different ways. 'We'll meet at Larry's to-morrow!' said Fatty. 'In the garden if it's fine. Cheerio!'

Pip and Bets biked down their lane and into their drive. 'I'm jolly thirsty,' said Pip. 'I wonder if Gladys would give us some ice out of the frig to put into a jug of water. I feel like a drink of iced water, I'm so hot.'

'Well, don't ask Mrs. Moon,' said Bets. 'She's sure to say no!'

They went to find Gladys. She wasn't in the kitchen, for they peeped in at the window to see. She wasn't upstairs either, for they went up and called her. Their mother heard them and came out of the study to greet them as they ran downstairs again.

'Did you have a lovely day?' she said. 'I was pleased it was so fine for you.

'Yes, a super day,' said Pip. 'Mother, can we have a drink of iced water? We're melting!'

'Yes, if you like,' Mrs.Hilton said. They shot off to the kitchen. They peeped in. Mrs. Moon was there knitting.

'What do you want?' she said, looking unexpectedly amiable.

'Just some iced water, please,' said Pip. 'But we weren't going to ask you for it, Mrs. Moon. We were going to ask Gladys. We didn't want to bother you.'

'No bother,' said Mrs. Moon, getting up. 'I'll get it.'

'Is Gladys out?' asked Bets.

'Yes,' said Mrs. Moon shortly. 'Now, take these ice-cubes quick, and slip them into a jug. That's right.'

'But it isn't Glady's day out, is it?' said Pip, surprised. 'She went the day before yesterday.'

'There now—you've dropped an ice-cube!' said Mrs.

Moon. 'Well, I'm no good at chasing ice-cubes round the kitchen floor, so you must get it yourselves.'

Bets giggled as Pip tried to get the cold slippery ice-cube off the floor. He rinsed it under the tap and popped it into the jug.

'Thanks, Mrs. Moon,' he said and carried the jug and two glasses up to the playroom.

'Mrs. Moon didn't seem to want to talk about Gladys, did she?' said Pip. 'Funny.'

'Pip—you don't think Gladys has left, do you?' suddenly said Bets. "I do hope she hasn't. I did like her.'

'Well—we can easily find out,' said Pip. 'Let's go and peep in her bedroom. If her things are there we'll know she's just out for a while and is coming back.'

They went along the landing to the little room that Gladys had. They opened the door and peeped in. They stared in dismay.

Every single thing that had belonged to Gladys had gone! Her brush and comb, her tooth-brush, and the little blue night-dress case she had embroidered at school for herself. There was nothing at all to show that the girl had been there for a month or two.

'Yes—she *has* gone!' said Bets. 'Well, why didn't Mother tell us? Or Mrs. Moon? What's all the mystery?'

'It's jolly funny,' said Pip. 'Do you think she stole any-thing? She seemed so nice. I liked her.'

'Let's go and ask Mother,' said Bets. So they went down to the study. But their mother was not there. They were just turning to go out when Pip's sharp eyes caught sight of something lying under a chair. He picked it up.

It was a large black woollen glove. He stared at it, trying to remember who wore black woollen gloves.

'Whose is it?' asked Bets. 'Look—isn't that a name inside?'

Pip looked—and the name he saw there made him stare hard. On a little tab was printed in marking ink, five letters: 'T. GOON.'

'T. GOON! Theophilus Goon!' said Pip, in surprise. 'Golly! What was old Clear-Orf here for today? He came here and sat in this study, and left a glove behind. No wonder Mother said she had important things to do if she had old Clear-Orf coming for a meeting! But why did he come?'

Bets burst into a loud wail. 'He's taken Gladys to prison! I know he has! Gladys has gone to prison, and I did like her so much.'

'Shut up, idiot!' said Pip. 'Mother will hear you.'

Mrs. Hilton came quickly into the study, thinking that Bets must surely have hurt herself. 'What's the matter dear?' she asked.

'Mother! Mr. Goon's taken Gladys to prison, hasn't he?' wept Bets. 'But I'm sure she didn't steal or anything. I'm sure she didn't. She was n-n-nice!'

'Bets, don't be silly,' said her mother. 'Of *course* Mr. Goon hasn't done anything of the sort.'

'Well, why was he here then?' demanded Pip.

'How do you know he was?' said his mother.

'Because of this,' said Pip, and he held out the large woollen glove. 'That's Mr. Goon's glove. So we know he has been here in the study—and as Gladys is gone we feel pretty certain Mr. Goon's had something to do with her go-ing.'

'Well, he hasn't,' said Mrs. Hilton. 'She was very upset about something to-day and I let her go home to her aunt.'

'Oh,' said Pip. 'Then why did Mr. Goon come to see you, Mother?'

'Really, Pip, it's no business of yours,' said his mother, quite crossly. 'I don't want you prying into it either. I know you all fancy yourselves as detectives, but this is nothing whatever to do with you, and I'm not going to have you mixed up in any of your so-called mysteries again.'

'Oh—is there a mystery then?' said Bets. 'And is old Clear-Orf trying to solve it? Oh Mother, you might tell us, you might!'

'It's nothing whatever to do with you,' said Mrs. Hilton firmly. 'Your father and I have discussed something with Mr. Goon, that's all.'

'Has he been complaining about us?' asked Pip.

'No, for a wonder he hasn't,' said his mother. 'Stop howl-ing, Bets. There's nothing to wail about.'

Bets dried her eyes. 'Why did Gladys go?' she said. 'I want her to come back.'

'Well, maybe she will,' said her mother. 'I can't tell you why she went, except that whe was upset about something, that's all. It's her own private business.'

Mrs. Hilton went out of the room. Pip looked at Bets, and slipped his hand into the enormous black glove. 'Golly, what a gaint of a hand old Clear-Orf must have,' he said. 'I do wonder why he was here, Bets. It was something to do with Gladys, I'm certain.

'Let's go up and tell Fatty,' said Bets. 'He'll know what
to do. Why is everything being kept such a secret? And oh, I
do hate to think of Clear-Orf sitting here talking with Mother,
and grinning to think we were not to know anything about
it!'

They couldn't go up to Fatty's that evening, because Mrs.
Hilton suddenly decided she wanted to wash their hair. 'But
mine's quite clean,' protested Pip.

'It looks absolutely black,' said his mother. 'What *have*
you been doing to it to-day, Pip? Standing on your head in a
heap of soot, or something?'

'Can't we have our heads washed to-morrow
night?' said Bets. But it wasn't a bit of good. It had to be
then and there. So it wasn't until the next day
that Pip and Bets were able to see Fatty. He was at Larry's,
of course, because they had all arranged to
meet there.

'I say,' began Pip, 'a funny thing's happened at our house.
Old Clear-Orf went there yesterday to see my father and
mother   about   something   so   mysterious
that nobody will tell us what it was! And Gladys, our nice
housemaid, has gone home, and we can't find
out exactly why. And look—here's a glove Goon left behind.'

Every one examined it. 'It might be a valuable clue,' said
Bets.

'Idiot!' said Pip. 'I keep telling you you can't
have clues before you've got a mystery to solve.
Besides, how could Goon's glove be a clue! You're

a baby.'

'Well—it *was* a clue to his presence there in your study yesterday,' said Fatty, seeing Bets, eyes fill with tears. 'But I say—it's all a bit funny, isn't it? Do you think Goon is on to some mystery we haven't heard about, but which your mother and father know of, Pip, and don't want us to be mixed up in? I know that your parents weren't very pleased at that adventure we had in the Christmas hols. I wouldn't be a bit surprised if there isn't something going on that we children are to be kept out of!

There was a silence. Put like that it seemed extremely likely. What a shame to be kept out of a mystery when they were such very good detectives!

'What's more, I think the mystery's got something to do with Glady's,' said Fatty. 'Fancy! To think there may have been something going on under our very noses and we didn't know it! There we were snooping about in barns and sheds and all the time there was a mystery in Pip's own house!

'Well—we'll jolly well find out what it is!' said Larry. 'And what's more if Goon is on to it, we'll be on to it too, and we'll get to the bottom of things before *he* does! I bet he'd like to do us down just once, so that Inspector Jenks would pat him on the back, and not us, for a change.'

'How are we going to find out anything?' asked Daisy. 'We can't possibly ask Mrs. Hilton. She'd just shut us up.'

'I'll go down and tackle Goon,' said Fatty, much to every one's admiration. 'I'll take his glove back, and pretend to know lots more that I do—and maybe he'll let out something.'

'Yes—you go,' said Pip. 'But wait a bit—he thinks you're

in China!'

'Oh, I've come back now after solving the case there very quickly!' laughed Fatty. 'Give me the glove, Pip. I'll go along now. Come with me, Buster. Goon isn't likely to lose his temper with me quite so violently if you're there!'

5 THE 'NONNIMUS' LETTER

FATTY rode off on his bicycle, Buster in the basket. He came to Mr. Goon's house, and went to knock at the door. It was opened by Mrs. Cockles, who cleaned for Mr. Goon, and for the Hiltons as well. She knew Fatty and liked him.

'Is Mr. Goon in?' asked Fatty. 'Oh good. I'll come in and see him then. I've got some property to return to him.'

He sat down in the small, hot parlour. Mrs. Cockles went to fetch the policeman. He was mending a puncture in his bicycle, out in his backyard. He put his coat on and came to see who wanted him.

His eyes nearly fell out of his head when he saw Fatty. 'Lawks!' he said. 'I thought you was in foreign parts!'

'Oh—I solved that little mystery out there,' said Fatty. 'Didn't take me long! Just a matter of an emerald necklace or so. Pity you didn't come out with me to Tippylooloo, Mr. Goon. You'd have enjoyed eating rice with chop-sticks.'

Mr. Goon was sure he would have enjoyed no such thing. 'Pity you didn't stay away longer,' he grumbled. 'Where you are, there's trouble. I know that by now. What you want this morning?'

'Well—er—Mr. Goon, you remember that little matter you went to see Mr. and Mrs. Hilton about yesterday?'said Fatty, pretending to know a great deal more than he actually did. Mr. Goon looked surprised.

'Now look-ere,' he said. 'Who's been telling you about that? You wasn't to know anything, any of you, see?'

'You can't keep things like that secret,' said Fatty.

'Things like what?' asked Mr. Goon, pretending he didn't know what Fatty was talking about.

'Well—things like you-know-what,' said Fatty, going all mysterious. I know you're going to set to work on that little matter, Mr. Goon, and I wish you luck. I hope, for poor Gladys's sake, you'll soon get to the bottom of the matter.'

This was quite a shot in the dark, but it seemed to surprise Mr. Goon very much. He blinked at Fatty out of his bulging frog-eyes.

'Who told you about that there letter?' he suddenly said.

'Oho,' thought Fatty, 'so it's something to do with a letter!' He spoke aloud.

'Ah, I have ways and means of finding out these things, Mr, Goon. We'd like to help you if we can.'

Mr. Goon suddenly lost his temper,and his face went brick-red. 'I don't want none of your help!' he shouted. 'I've had enough of it! Help? Interference is what I call it! Can't I manage a case on my own without all you children butting in? You keep out of it! Mrs. Hilton, she promised me she wouldn't say nothing to any of you, nor, show you that letter either. She didn't want you poking your noses in no more than I did. Anyway, this is a case for the police not for little busy-bodies like you! Clear-Orf now, and don't let me see you messing about any more.'

'I thought perhaps you would like your glove, Mr.Goon,' said Fatty politely, and he held out the policeman's big glove. 'You left it behind you yesterday.'

Mr. Goon snatched at it angrily. Buster growled. 'You and that dog of yours!' muttered Mr.Goon. 'Tired to death of both of you I am. Clear-Orf!'

Fatty cleared off. He was pleased with the result of his interview with Mr. Goon, but very puzzled. Mr. Goon had given a few things away—about that letter, for instance. But what letter? What could have been in a letter to cause this mystery? Was it something to do with Gladys? Was it *her* letter?

Puzzling out all these things Fatty cycled back to the others. He soon told them what he had learnt.

'I think possibly Mrs. Moon may know something,' he said. 'Bets, couldn't you ask her? If you just sort of prattled to her, she might tell you something.'

'I don't prattle,' said Bets indignantly. 'And I don't expect she'd tell me anything at all. I'm sure she's in this business of keeping everything secret from us. She wouldn't even tell us yesterday that Gladys had gone.'

'Well, anyway, see what you can do,' said Fatty. 'She's fond of knitting, isn't she? Well, haven't you got a bit of tangled up knitting you could take down to her and ask her to undo for you—pick up the stitches or whatever you call it? Then you could sort of prat . . . er—talk to her about Gladya and Goon and so on.'

'I'll try,' said Bets 'I'll go downstairs to her this afternoon when she's sitting down resting. She doesn't like me messing about in the morning.'

So that afternoon Bets went down to the kitchen with some very muddled knitting indeed. She had been planning earnestly what to say to Mrs. Moon, but she felt very nervous. Mrs. Moon could be very snappy if she wanted to.

There was no one in the kitchen. Bets sat down in the rocking-chair there. She always liked that old chair. She rocked herself to and fro.

From the back-yard came two voices. One was Mrs. Moon's and the other was Mrs. Cockles's. Bets hardly listened—but then she suddenly sat up.

'Well, what I say is, if a girl gets a nasty letter telling her things she wants to forget, and no name at the bottom of the letter, it's enough to give any one a horrid shock!' came Mrs. Moon's voice. 'And a nasty, yes right-down nasty thing it is to do! Writing letters and putting no name at the bottom.'

'Yes, that's a coward's trick all right,' said Mrs. Cockles's cheerful voice. 'You mark my words, Mrs. Moon, there'll be more of those nonnimus letters, or whatever they calls them—those sort of letter-writer don't just stop at the one person. No they've got too much spite to use up on one person, they'll write more and more. Why, *you* might get one next!'

'Poor Gladys was right-down upset,' said Mrs. Moon. 'Cried and cried, she did. I made her show me the letter. All in capital letters it was, not proper writing. And I said to her, I said, "Now look here, my girl, you go straight off to your mistress and tell her about this. She'll do her best for you, she will." And I pushed her off to Mrs. Hilton.'

'Did she give her her notice?' asked Mrs. Cockles.

'No,' said Mrs. Moon. 'She showed Mr. Hilton the letter, and he rang up Mr. Goon. That silly, fussing fellow! What do they want to bring *him* in for!'

'Oh, he's not so bad,' sais Mrs. Cockles's cheerful voice. 'Just hand me that broom, will you? Thanks. He's all right if he's treated rough. I don't stand no nonsense from him, I don't. I've cleaned for him now for years, and he's never had a harsh word for me. But my, how he hates those children!'

'Ah, that's another thing,' said Mrs. Moon. 'When Mr. Hilton told him about this here letter, he was that pleased to think those kids knew nothing about it—and he made Master and Mistress promise they'd not let those five interfere. And they promised. I was there, holding up poor Gladys, and I heard every word. "Mrs. Hilton," he said, "Mrs. Hilton, madam, this is not a case for children to interfere in and I must request you, in the name of the law, to keep this affair to yourselves."'

'Lawks!' said Mrs. Cockles. 'He can talk grand when he likes, can't he? I reckon, Mrs. Moon maybe there's been more of these letters than we know. Well, well—so poor Gladys went home, all upset-like. And who's going to come in her place, I wonder? Or will she be coming back?'

'Well, it's my belief she'd better keep away from this village now,' said Mrs.Moon. 'Tongues will wag, you know. I've got a niece who can come next week, so it won't matter much if she keeps away.'

'What about a cup of tea?' said Mrs. Cockles. 'I'm that thirsty with all this cleaning. These rugs look a fair treat now, Mrs. Moon.'

Bets fled as soon as she heard footsteps coming in at the scullery door. Her knitting almost tripped her up as she went. She ran up the stairs and into the playroom, painting. Pip was there, reading and waiting for her.

'Pip! I 've found out everything, simply everything!' cried Bets. 'And there *is* a mystery to solve—a kind we haven't had before.'

Sounds of laughter floated up from the drive. It was the others coming. 'Wait a bit,' said Pip, excited. 'Wait till the others come up. Then you can tell the whole lot. Golly, you must have done well, Bets!'

The others saw at once from Bets' face that she had news for them. 'Good old Bets!' said Fatty. 'Go on, Betsy. spill the beans!'

Bets told them everything. 'Somebody wrote a nonnimus letter to Gladys,' she said. 'What *is* a nonnimus letter, Fatty?'

Fatty grinned. 'You mean an *anonymous* letter, Bets,' he said.' A letter sent without the name of the sender at the bottom—usually a beastly cowardly sort of letter, saying things that the writer wouldn't dare to say to any one's face. So poor Gladys got an anonymous letter, did she?'

'Yes,' said Bets. 'I don't know what it said though. It upset her. Mrs. Moon got out of her what it was and made her go and see Mother and Daddy about it. And they rang up Mr. Goon.'

'And he came popping along, his eyes bulging with delight because he'd got a mystery to solve that we didn't know about !' said Fatty. 'So there's an anonymous letter-writer somewhere here, is there? A nasty, cowardly letter-writer—well, here's our mystery, Find-Outers ! WHO is the writer of the "nonnimus" letters ?'

'We shall never be able to find that out,' said Dasiy. ' How on earth could we ?'

We must make plans,' said Fatty. 'We must search for clues!' Bets' face lighted up at once. She loved hunting for clues. 'We must make a list of suspects—people who could do it and would. We must...'

'We haven't got to work with Goon, have we ?' said Pip. 'We don't need to let him know we know, do we?'

'Well—he already thinks we know most of this,' said Fatty. 'I don't see why we shouldn't tell him we know as much as he does, and not tell him how we've found out, and make him think we know a lot more than we do. That'll make him sit up a bit!'

So, the next time that the Five Find-Outers met the police-man, they stopped to speak to him.

'How are you getting on with this difficult case ?' asked Fatty gravely. It—er—it abounds with such strange clues, doesn't it ?'

Mr. Goon hadn't discovered a single clue, and he was as-tonished and annoyed to hear that there were apparently things the children knew and he didn't. He stared at them.

'You tell me your clues you've found,' he said at last. ' We'll swap clues. It beats me how you know about this af-fairs. You wasn't to know a thing, not a thing.'

'We know much more than you think,' said Fatty solemnly. 'A very difficult and—er—enthralling case.'

'You tell me your clues,' said Mr. Goon again. 'We'd bet-ter swap clues, like I said. Better help one another than hinder, I always say.'

'Now, where did I put those clues?' said Fatty, diving into his capacious pockets. He brought out a live white rat and stared at it. 'Was this a clue or not?' he asked the others. 'I can't remember.'

It was impossible not to giggle. Bets went off into a de-lighted explosion. Mr. Goon glared.

'You clear-off,' he said majestically. 'Making a joke of everything ! Call yourself a detective ! Gah!'

'What a lovely word !' said Bets, as they all walked off, giggling. 'Gah! Gah, Pip ! Gah, Fatty!'

Fatty brought out a live white rat

6 THE FIND-OUTERS MAKE THEIR FIRST PLANS

EVERY one went to tea at Fatty's that day. Mrs. Trotteville was out, so the five children had tea in Fatty's crowded little den. It was more crowded than ever now that Fatty had got various disguises and wigs. The children exclaimed in delight over a blue-and-white striped butcher-boy's apron and a lift-boy's suit complete with peaked cap.

'But, Fatty, whenever could you disguise your self as a lift-boy ?' asked Larry.

'You never know,' said Fatty. 'You see, I can only get disguises that do for a boy. If I were a grown-up I could get dozens and dozens—a sailor's suit, a postman's even a policeman's. But I'm a bit limited, being a boy.'

Fatty also had a bookcase crammed full of detective stories. He read every one he could find. 'I pick up quite a lot of hints that way,' he said. 'I think Sherlock Holmes was one of the best detectives. Golly, he had some fine mysteries to solve. I don't believe even I could have solved all of them!'

'You're a conceited creature,' said Larry, trying on the red wig. He looked very startling in it. 'How do you put those freckles on that you had with this?' he asked.

'Grease-paint,' said Fatty. 'There are my grease-paints over there—what actors use for make-up, you know. One day I'm going to make myself up as a monster and give you all a fright.'

'Oh—do give old Clear-Orf a scare too!' begged Bets.

'Let me try on that wig, Larry; do let me.'

'We really ought to be making our plans to tackle this mystery,' said Fatty, taking a beautiful gold pencil out of his pocket. Pip stared.

'I say! Is that gold ?'

'Yes.' said Fatty airily. 'I won it last term for the best essay. Didn't I tell you ? It was a marvellous essay, all about...'

'All right, all right,' said Larry and Pip together. 'We'll take your word for it, Fatty!'

'I had a marvellous report again,' said Fatty. 'Did you, Pip?'

'You know I didn't,' said Pip. 'You heard my mother say so. Shut up, Fatty.'

'Let's talk about out new mystery,' said Daisy, seeing that a quarrel was about to flare up. 'Write down some notes, Fatty. Let's get going.'

'I was just about to,' said Fatty, rather pompously. He printed in beautiful small letters a heading to the page in the lovely leather notebopok he held. The others looked to see what he had printed:

MYSTERY NO. 4.   BEGUN APRIL 5TH.

'Ooh—that looks fine,' said Bets.

'CLUES' was the next thing printed by Fatty, over the page.

'But we haven't got any,' said Pip.

'We soon shall have,' said Fatty. He turned over the page. 'SUSPECTS' was what he printed there.

'We don't know any of those yet either,' said Daisy. 'And I'm sure I don't know how we're going to find any.'

'Leave it to me,' said Fatty. 'We'll soon have something to work on.'

'Yes, but what?' said Pip. 'I mean, it's no use looking for footprints or cigarette-ends or dropped hankies or anything like that. There's just nothing at all we can find for clues.'

'There's one very important thing,' said Fatty.

'What's that?' said every one.

'That anonymous letter,' said Fatty. 'It's most important we should get a glimpse of it. Most important!'

'Who's got it?' asked Larry.

'My mother might have it,' said Pip.

'More likely Gladys has got it, said Fatty. 'That's the first thing we must do. Go and see Gladys, and ask her if she knows or guesses who could have written her that letter. We must also find out what's in it.'

'Let's go now,' said Pip, who always liked to rush off as soon as anything had been decided.

'Right. You take us,' said Fatty. Pip looked rather blank.

'But I don't know where Gladys lives,' he said.

'Ha, I thought you didn't', said Fatty. 'Well, Pip, you must find out. That's the first thing we've got to do—find out where Gladys lives.'

'I could ask Mother,' said Pip doubtfully.

'Now don't be such a prize idiot,' said Fatty at once. 'Use your brains! You know jolly well your parents don't want us mixed up in this mystery, and we've got to keep it dark that we're finding out things. Don't on any account ask your mother anything—or Mrs. Moon either.'

'Well, but how am I to find out then?' said Pip, looking bewildered.

'I know a way, I know a way!' sang out Bets suddenly. 'Gladys lent me a book once and I didn't have time to give it her back before she left. I could go to Mrs. Moon and tell her, and ask her for Gladys's address so that I sould send the book on to her.'

'Clever girl!' said Fatty. 'You're coming on well, you are, Bets! Perhaps you'd better handle this, and not Pip'

'I've got an idea too now,' said Pip, rather sulkily.

'What?' said Bets.

'Well—if I got a bit of paper and stuck it in an envelope, and wrote Gladys's name and our address on it and posted it—Mother would re-address it and I could hang about and see what it was, when, she puts the letter on the hall-stand to be posted,' said Pip.

'Yes, that's a very fine idea too,' said Fatty. 'Couldn't have thought of a much better one myself. Go to the top of the class, Pip.'

Pip grinned. 'Well—both Bets and I will carry out our ideas,' he said, 'and surely one of us will get Gladys's address!'

'Here's a bit of paper and an envelope,' said Fatty. 'But disguise your writing, Pip.'

'Why?' said Pip, surprised.

'Well—seeing that yout mother gets a letter from you every single week when you're away at boarding-school, it's likely she *might* recognize your writing and wonder why on earth you were writing to Gladys when she was gone!' said Fatty, in a very patient, but rather tired voice.

'Fatty thinks of everything!' said Daisy admiringly. Pip saw the point at once, but doubted very much if he could disguise his writing properly.

'Here—give it to me. I'll do it,' said Fatty, who was apparently able to disguise his writing as easily as he could disguise his appearance and his voice. He took the envelope, and, to the children's enormous admiration, wrote Gladys's name and Pip's address in small, extremely grown-up handwriting, quite unlike his own.

'There you are,' he said. 'Elementary, my dear Pip!'

'Marvellous, Mr. Sherlock Holmes!' said Pip. 'Honestly, Fatty, you're a wonder. How many different writings can you do?'

'Any amount,' said Fatty. 'What to see the writing of a poor old charwoman? Here it is !'

He wrote a few words in a scrawling, untidy writing. 'Oh, it's just like Mrs. Cockles's writing!' cried Bets in delight. 'Sometimes she puts out a notice for the milkman—"TWO PINTS' or something like that—and her writing is just like that!'

'Now write like old Clear-Orf,' said Larry. 'Go on! What does *he* write like?'

'Well, I've seen his writing, so I know what it's like,' said Fatty, 'but if I hadn't seen it I'd know too—he'd be bound to write like this. . . .'

He wrote a sentence or two in a large, flourishing hand with loops and tails to the letters—an untidy, would-be impressive hand—yes, just like Mr.Goon's writing.

'Fatty, you're always doing something surprising,' said Bets, with a sigh. 'There's nothing you can't do. I wish I was like you.'

'You be like yourself. You couldn't be nicer,' said Fatty,

giving the little girl a squeeze. Bets was pleased. She liked and admired Fatty very much indeed.

'You know, once last term I thought I'd try out a new handwriting on my form-master,' said Fatty. 'So I made up a marvellous handwriting, very small and neat and pointed, with most of the letters leaning backwards—and old Tubbs wouldn't pass it—said I'd got some one to do that prep for me, and made me do it all again.'

'Poor Fatty,' said Bets.

'Well, the next time I gave my prep in, it was written in old Tubbs, own handwriting,' said Fatty, with a grin. 'Golly, it gave him a start to see a prep all done in his own writing!'

'What *did* he say?' asked Pip.

'He said, "And who's done this prep for you this time, Trotteville?" And I said, " My goodness, sir, it looks as if *you* have!"' said Fatty. The others roared with laughter. Whether Fatty's school tales were true or not, they were always funny.

Pip slipped the blank piece of paper into the envelope that Fatty had addressed and stuck it down. He took the stamp that Fatty offered him and put it on.

'There!' he said. 'I'll post it on my way home to-night. It'll catch the half-past six post and it will be there to-morrow morning. Then if I don't manage to spot the re-addressed letter my name isn't Pip.'

'Well, it isn't,' said Bets. 'It's Philip.'

'Very funny!' said Pip. 'I don't think!'

'Now don't squabble, you two,' said Fatty. 'Well, we've done all we can for the moment. Let's have a game. I'll teach you Woo-hoo-colly-wobbles.'

'Gracious! Whatever's that?' said Bets.

It was a game involving much woo-hoo-ing and groaning and rolling over and over. Soon all the children were reduced to tears of mirth. Mrs. Trotteville sent up to say that if anybody was ill they were to go down and tell her, but if they were just playing, would they please go out into the garden, down to the very bottom.

'Oooh. I didn't know your mother was back,' said Pip, who had really let himself go. 'We'd better stop. What an awful game this is, Fatty.'

'I say—it's almost half-past six!' said Larry. 'If you're going to post that letter, you'd better go, young Pip. Brush yourself down, for goodness sake. You look awful.'

'Gah!' said Pip, remembering Mr. Goon's last exclamation. He brushed himself down, and re-tied his tie. 'Come on, Bets,' he said. 'Well, so long, you others—we'll tell you Gladys's address to-morrow, and then we'll go and see her and examine our first clue—the "nonnimus" letter!'

He ran down the path with Bets. Fatty leaned out of the window of his den and yelled, 'Oy! You're a fine detective! You've forgotten the letter!'

'So I have!' said Pip and tore back for it. Fatty dropped it down. Pip caught it and ran off again. He and Bets tore to the pillar-box at the corner and were just in time to catch the postman emptying the letters from the inside.

'One more!' said Pip. 'Thanks, postman! Come on, Bets. We'll try out your book-idea as soon as we get home.'

7 DISAPPOINTMENT FOR PIP AND BETS

BETS flew to find the book that Gladys had lent her, as soom as she got home. She found it at once. It was an old school prize, called *The Little Saint*. Bets had been rather bored with it. 'The Little Saint' had been a girl much too good to be true. Bets preferred to read about naughty, lively children.

She wrapped the book up carefully, and then went down to say good-night to her mother. Mrs. Hilton was reading in the drawing-room.

'Come to say good-night, Bets?' she said, looking at the clock. 'Did you have a nice time at Fatty's?'

'Yes! We played his new game, Woo-hoo-colly-wobbles,' said Bets. 'It was fun.'

'I expect it was noisy and ridiculous if it was anything to do with Frederick,' said her mother. 'What's that you've got, Bets?'

'Oh Mother, it's a book that Gladys lent me,' said Bets. 'I was going to ask Mrs.Moon her address so that I could send it to her. Could I have a stamp, Mother?'

'You don't need to ask Mrs. Moon,' said her mother. 'I'll see that Gladys gets it.'

'Oh,' said Bets. 'Well—I'll just put her address on it. I've written her name. What's her address, Mother ?'

'I'll write it,' said Mrs.Hilton. 'Now don't stand there putting off time, Bets. Go up to bed. Leave the parcel here.'

'Oh, do let me just write the address,' said poor Bets, feeling that her wonderful idea was coming to nothing, and that it wasn't fair. 'I feel like writing, Mother.'

'Well, it must be for the first time in your life then!' said Mrs.Hilton. 'You've always said how much you hate writing before. Go up to bed, Bets, now.'

Bets had to go. She left the book on the table by her mother, feeling rather doleful. But perhaps Pip would see the address later on in the evening, if her mother wrote it on the parcel.

Pip said he'd keep an eye open. Anyway, what did it matter? His own letter would come in the morning and they'd soon find out the right address.

He saw the book on the table when he went down ready for dinner, cleaned and brushed. He read the name on the wrapping-paper... but there was no address there yet.

'Shall I write Gladys's address for you, Mother?' he asked politely. 'Just to save you time.'

'I can't imagine why you and Bets are so anxious to do a little writing to-night!' said Mrs. Hilton, looking up from her book. 'No, Pip. I can't remember it off-hand. Leave it.'

So it had to be left. Pip was glad to think his letter was coming in the morning. He was sure that had been a better idea than Bets'!

Pip was down early next morning, waiting for the postman. He took all the letters out of the box and put them by his mother's plate. His own was there, addressed in Fatty's disguised handwriting.

'There's a letter for Gladys, Mother,' said Pip, at breakfast-time. 'We'll have to re-address it.'

'My dear boy, you don't need to tell me that!' said Mrs. Hilton.

'Did you put the address on my parcel?' asked Bets, attacking her boiled egg hungrily.

'No. I couldn't remember it last night,' said Mrs. Hilton, reading her letters.

'Shall Pip and I take the letters and the parcel to the post for you this morning?' asked Bets, thinking this was really a very good idea.

'If you like,' said Mrs.Hilton. Bets winked at Pip. Now things would be easy! They could both see the address they wanted.

A telephone call came for Mrs. Hilton after breakfast, whilst the children were hanging about waiting to take the letters. Mrs. Moon answered it. She went in to Mrs. Hilton.

'There's a call for you, Mam,' she said.

'Who is it?' asked Mrs. Hilton. Pip and Bets were most astonished to see Mrs. Moon winking and nodding mysteriously to their mother, but not saying any name. However, Mrs. Hilton seemed to understand all right.She got up and went to the telephone, shutting the door behind her so that the children could not follow without being noticed.

'Well—who's on the phone that Mother doesn't want us to know about?' said Pip, annoyed. 'Did you see how mysterious Mrs. Moon was, Bets?'

'Yes,' said Bets. 'Can't we just open the door a bit and listen, Pip?'

'No,' said Pip, 'We really can't. Not if Mother doesn't want us to hear.

Their mother came back after a minute or two. She didn't say who had telephoned to her and the children didn't dare to ask.

'Shall we go to the post-office now?' said Pip, at last.

'We're ready.'

'Yes. There are the letters over there,' said Mrs. Hilton.

'What about my parcel for Gladys?' said Bets.

'Oh, that doesn't need to go—nor the letter for her,' said Mrs. Hilton. 'Somebody's going to see her to-day and he will take them. That will save putting a stamp on the parcel.'

'Who's going to see Gladys?' asked Pip. 'Can we go too? I'd like to see Gladys again.'

'Well, you can't,' said Mrs. Hilton. 'And please don't start trying to find out things, Pip, because, as I've already told you, this is nothing whatever to do with you. You can take the other letters to the post for me. Go now and you will catch the ten o'clock post.'

Pip and Bets went off rather sulkily. Bets was near tears. 'It's too bad, Pip,' she said, when they got out-of-doors, 'we had such good ideas—and now they're no use at all!'

'We'll post the letters and then go up and see Fatty,' said Pip gloomily. 'I expect he'll think we ought to have done better. He always thinks he can do things so marvellously.'

'Well, so he can,' said Bets loyally. 'Let *me* post the letters, Pip. Here's the post office.'

'Here you are then. What a baby you are to like posing letters still!' said Pip. Bets slipped them into the letter-box and they turned to go up to Fatty's house. He was at home, reading a new detective book.

'Our ideas weren't any good,' said Pip. He told Fatty what had happened. Fatty was unexpectedly sympathetic.'

'That was hard luck,' he said. 'You both had jolly fine ideas, and it was only a bit of bad luck that stopped them having their reward. Now—who is it that is going to see

Gladys to-day?'

'Mother said it was a "he," said Pip. 'She said, "Somebody's going to see Gladys to-day, and *he* will take them!"

'That's easy then,' said Fatty briskly. '*He* can only mean one person—and that's old Clear-Orf! Well, now we know what to do.'

'*I* don't know,' said Pip, still gloomy. 'You always seem to know everything, Fatty.'

'Brains, my dear fellow, brains!' said Fatty. 'We'll, look here—if it's Goon that's going to see Gladys, we can wait about and follow him, can't we? He'll go on his bike, I expect—well, we can go on ours! Easy!'

Pip and Bets cheered up. The idea of stalking old Clear-Orf was a pleasing one. They would have the fun of doing that, and would find out too where Gladys lived. Yes, to-day looked much more exciting now.

'You go and tell Larry and Daisy,' said Fatty. 'We shall have to keep a watch on old Goon's house so that we know when he leaves. I vote we ask our mothers for food again, so that we can go off at any time and come back when we like.'

'I'm going to buy Gladys some sweets,' said Bets. 'I like her.'

'It would be a good idea if we all took her some little present,' said Fatty thoughtfully. ' Sort of show we were sorry for her and were on her side, so that she'll be more willing to talk.'

'Well, I'll go and tell Larry and Daisy to get out their bikes and bring food along,' said Pip. 'I'd better hurry in case old Clear- Orf goes this morning. Bets, you'd better come back home with me too, and get your bike, because we'll both need them. Then we'll go to Larry's and then we'll buy some little things for Gladys.'

'I'll go and keep a watch on Goon's house in case he starts off before you're back,' said Fatty. 'I'll just get some sandwiches first. See you round the corner from Goon's!'

In about half an hour's time Larry, Daisy, Bets, and Pip were all with Fatty, round the corner near Clear-Orf's house, complete with sandwiches and little presents for Gladys. There had been no sign of Goon.

But in about ten minutes' time, Larry, who was on guard, gave a whistle. That was the signal to say that Goon was departing somewhere. He was on his bicycle, a portly, clumsy figure with short legs ending in enormous boots that rested on pedals looking absurdly small.

He set off down the road that led to the river. 'May be going across in the ferry!' panted Fatty, pedalling furiously. 'Come on! Don't all tear round the corners together in case he spots us. I'll always go first.'

But unfortunately all that Mr. Goon had gone to do down the river-lane was to leave a message with the farmer there. He was the farmer in the field and called out the message to him, then quickly turned his bicycle round and cycled back up the lane again. He came round the corner very quickly and found himself wobbing in the middle of the Five Find-Outers!

He came off with a crash. The children jumped off and Fatty tried to help him up, whilst Buster, jumping delightedly out of Fatty's basket, yelped in delight.

'Hurt yourself, Mr.Goon?' asked Fatty politely. 'Here,

let me give you a heave up.'

'You let me alone!' said Mr. Goon angirly. 'Riding five abreast like that in a narrow lane! What do you mean by it!'

'So sorry, Mr. Goon,' said Fatty. Pip gave a giggle. Old Clear-Orf looked so funny, trying to disentangle himself form his bicycle.'

Yes, you laugh at me, you cheeky little toad!' roared Mr.Goon. 'I'll tell of you, you see if I don't. I'll be seeing your Ma this morning and I'll put in a complaint. I'm going right along there now.'

Fatty brushed Mr. Goon down so smartly that the policeman jumped aside. 'You're all dusty, Mr. Goon,' said Fatty anxiously. 'You can't go to Mrs. Hilton's in this state. Just a few more whacks and you'll be all right!'

'Wait till you get the whacks *you* want!' said Mr. Goon, putting his helmet on firmly. 'Never knew such children in me life! Nothing but trouble round every corner where you are! Gah!'

He rode off, leaving the children standing in the lane with their bicycles. 'Well, that was a bit of a nuisance bumping into him like that,' said Fatty. 'I didn't particularly want him to see any of us to-day. I don't want him to suspect we're on his track. Now let me see—he's off to collect those things of Gladys from your mother, Pip. There's no doubt about that. So all we've got to do now is to lie in wait for him somewhere and then follow him very carefully.'

'Let's go to the church corner,' said Pip. 'He's sure to pass there, wherever he goes. Come on!'

So off they went, and hid behind some trees, waiting for old Clear-Orf to show them the way to where Gladys lived.

IN about half an hour Mr. Goon came cycling along, and went right by the hidden children without seeing them

'Now listen!' said Fatty. 'It's no use us all tearing after him in a bunch because we'd be so easy to spot. I'll go first and keep a long way ahead. You follow, see? If I have to take a turning you may not know I'll tear a sheet out of my notebook and drop it the way I go.'

'It's windy to-day. Better hop off your bike and chalk one of those arrows on the road that gypsies always seem to make,' said Pip. 'Your bit of paper might blow away. Got any chalk, Fatty?'

'Of course!' said Fatty and took a piece out of his capacious pockets. 'Yes, that's a better idea. Good for you, Pip! Well, I'll get along in front of you now. Look, there goes old Clear-Orf panting up the hill in the distance. Looks as if he's going to take the main road.'

Fatty rode off, whistling. The others waited a little while and then rode after him. It was easy.to see him in the distance in the open country. But soon they came to where the road forked, and Fatty seemed nowhere in sight.

'Here you are! Here's his chalk arrow!' said Daisy, her sharp eyes spotting it at once, marked on the path at the side of one of the roads. 'This is the way!'

They rode on again. They rarely saw Fatty now, for he and Mr. Goon had left the main raod and were cycling down narrow, winding lanes. But at every doubtful fork or corner they saw his chalk mark.

'This is fun,' said Bets, who liked looking for the little

arrows. 'But oh dear—I hope it's not much farther!'

'Looks as if Gladys lives at Haycock Heath,'said Larry. 'This road leads there. My, here's a steep hill. Up we go! I bet old Fatty found it heavy going here, with Buster in his basket. Buster seems to weigh an awful lot when he's in a bicycle basket.'

At the top of the hill, just at a bend, Fatty was waiting for them. He looked excited.

'He's gone into the very last cottage of all!' he said. 'And isn't it good luck—it's got a notice with "Minerals" printed on it, in the window. That means lemonade or ginger-beer is sold there. We've got a fine excuse for going in, once Clear-Orf has gone.'

'Better get back into this other little lane here, hadn't we?' said Larry. 'I mean—if old Clear-Orf suddenly comes out, he'll find us!'

So they all wheeled their bicycles into a crooked, narrow little lane, whose trees met overhead and made a green tunnel. 'Must give old Buster a run,' said Fatty and lifted him out of the basket. But unfortunately a cat strolled down the lane, appearing suddenly from the hedge, and Buster immediately gave chase, barking joyfully. Cats and rabbits were his great delight.

The cat gave one look at Buster and decided to move quickly. She shot down the lane, and took a flying leap over the little wall surrounding the back-garden of the cottage into which Mr. Goon had disappeared. Buster tried to leap over too, and couldn't—but, using his brains as a Buster should, he decided that there must be another way in, and went to look for the front gate.

Then there was such a hurricane of barks and yowls, mixed with the terrified clucking of hens, that the children stood perrified. Out came Mr. Goon, with a sharp-nosed woman—and Gladys!

'You clear-orf!' yelled Mr. Goon to Buster. 'Bad dog, you! Clear-orf!'

With a bark of joy Buster flung himself at the policeman's ankles, and snapped happily at them.Mr. Goon kicked at him and let out a yell.

'It's that boy's dog! Get away, you! Now what's he doing here? Has that boy Frederick Trotteville been messing about up here, now?'

'Nobody's been here this morning but you,' said Gladys. 'Oh, Mr. Goon, don't kick at the dog like that. He wasn't doing much harm.'

It was quite plain that Buster meant to get a nip if he could. Fatty, feeling most annoyed at having to show himself, was forced to cycle out and yell to Buster.

'Hey, Buster! Come here, sir!'

Mr. Goon turned and gave Fatty a look that might have cowed a lion if Fatty had been a lion. But, being Fatty, he didn't turn a hair.

'Why, Mr. Goon!' he said, taking off his cap in a most aggravatingly polite manner, 'fancy seeing *you* here! Come for a little bike-ride too? Lovely day, isn't it?'

Mr. Goon almost exploded. 'Now what are *you* a-doing of here?' he demanded. 'You tell me that, see?'

'All I'm a-doing of at the moment is having a nice bike-ride,' answered Fatty cheerfully. 'What are *you* a-doing of, Mr. Goon? Having a ginger-beer? I see there's a card in the window. I think I'll have something to drink myself. It's a jolly hot day.'

And, to the other children's delight, and Mr. Goon's annoyance, Fatty strolled up the little front path and entered the door. Inside was a small table at which people could sit down to have their lemonade. Fatty sat down.

'You clear-orf out of here,' ordered Mr. Goon. 'I'm here on business, see? And I'm not having busy-bodies like you interfering. *I* know what you've come here for—snooping around—trying to find clues, and making nuisances of yourselves.'

'Oh, that reminds me,' said Fatty, beginning to feel in his pockets with a serious look, 'didn't we say we'd swap clues, Mr. Goon? Now where did I put that. . .'

'If you bring out that there white rat again I'll skin you alive!' boomed Mr. Goon, whose fingers were itching to box Fatty's ears.

'That white rat wasn't a clue after all,' said Fatty gravely. 'I made a mistake. That must have been a clue in another case I'm working on. Wait a bit—ah, this may be a clue!'

He fished a clothes-peg out of his pocket and looked at it solemnly. Mr. Goon, quite beside himself with rage, snatched at it, threw it down on the floor, and jumped on it! Then, looking as if he was going to burst, he took his bicycle by the handle-bars, and turned to Gladys and the other woman.

'Now don't you forget what I've said. And you let me hear as soon as anything else happens. Don't talk to nobody at all about this here case—them's my strict orders!'

He rode off, trying to look dignified, but unfortunately Buster flew after him, jumping up at his pedalling feet, so

that poor Mr. Goon wobbled dreadfully. As soon as he had
gone the children crowded up to Fatty, laughing.

'Oh, Fatty! How can you! One of these days old Clear-
Orf will kill you!'

Gladys and her aunt had been listening and watching in
surprise. Bets ran to Gladys and took her hand.

'Gladys! I *was* sorry you left! Do come back soon! Look,
I've brought you something!'

The sharp-nosed aunt made an impatient noise. 'I'll never
get to the shops this morning!' she said. 'I'm going right
away now, Gladys. See and get the dinner on in good time—
and mind you heed what the policeman said.'

Much to the children's relief, she put on an old hat and
scarf, and disappeared down the lane, walking quickly. They
were glad to see her go, for she looked rather bad-tempered.
They crowded round Gladys, who smiled and seemed very
pleased to see them.

'Gladys! We know something made you unhappy,' said
little Bets and pressed a bag of sweets in the girl's hand.
'We've come to say we're sorry and we've brought a few
little things for you. And please, please come back!'

Gladys seemed rather overcome. She took them all into
the little front-room and poured out some glasses of ginger-
beer for them.

'It's right down kind of you,' she said, in a tearful voice.
'Things aren't too easy— and my aunt isn't too pleased to
have me back. But I couldn't go on living in Peterswood
when I knew that—that—that . . . '

'That what?' asked Fatty gently.

'I'm not supposed to talk about it,' said Gladys.

'Well—we're only children. It can't matter talking to *us*,' said Bets. 'We all like you, Gladys. You tell us. Why, you never know, we might be able to help you!'

'There's nobody can help me,' said Galdys, and a tear ran down her cheek. She began to undo the little things the children had brought her—sweets, chocolate, a little brooch with G on, and two small hankies. She seemed very touched.

'It's kind of you,' she said. 'Goodness knows I want a bit of kindness now.'

'Why ?' asked Daisy. 'What's happened ? You tell us, Gladys. It will do you good to tell some one.'

'Well—it's like this,' said Gladys. 'There's something wrong I once did that I'm ashamed of now, see? And I had to go into a Home, and I liked it and I said I'd never do wrong again. Well, I left there and I got a job—with your mother, Master Pip and wasn't I happy working away there, and every-body treating me nice, and me forgetting all about the bad days!'

'Yes?' said Fatty, as Gladys paused. 'Go on, Gladys. Don't stop.'

'Then—then...' began Gladys again, and burst into tears. 'Somebody sent me a letter, and said, "We know you're a wrong-un, and you didn't ought to be in a good place with decent people. Clear out or we'll tell on you!"

'What a shame!' said Fatty. 'Who sent the letter?'

'I don't know that,' said Gladys. 'It was all in printed letters. Well, I was that upset I broke down in front of Mrs. Moon, and she took the letter from me and read it, and said I should ought to go to your mother, Master Pip, and tell her— but I didn't want to because I knew I'd lose my place. But she said, yes go, Mrs. Hilton would put things right for me. So I went, but I was that upset I couldn't speak a word.'

'Poor old Gladys!' said Daisy. 'But I'm sure Pip's mother was kind to you.'

'Oh yes—and shocked at the cruel letter,' said Gladys, wiping her eyes. 'And she said I could have two or three days off and go to my aunt to pull myself together, like—and she'd make inquiries and find out who wrote that letter—and stop them talking about me, so's I could have a chance. But my aunt wasn't too pleased to see me!'

'Why didn't you go to your father and mother, Gladys?' asked little Bets, who thought that surely they would have been the best friends for any girl of theirs who was unhappy.

'I couldn't,' said Gladys, and looked so sad that the children felt quite scared.

'Why—are they—are they—dead?' asked Bets.

'No. They're—they're in prison!' said poor Gladys and wept again. 'You see—they've always been dishonest folk—stealing and that—and they taught me to steal too. And the police got them, and when they found I was going into shops with my mother and taking things I didn't ought, they took me away and put me into a Home. I didn't know it was so wrong, you see—but now I do !'

The children were horrified that any one should have such bad parents. They stared at Gladys and tears ran down Bets' cheeks. She took Gladys's hand.

'You're good now, Gladys, aren't you?' said the little girl. 'You don't look bad. You're good now.'

'Yes—I've not done nothing wrong ever since,' said poor Gladys. 'Nor I never would now. They were so kind to me at the Home—you can't think! And I promised the Matron there I'd always do my best wherever I was, and I was so glad when they sent me to your mother's, Miss Bets. But there— they say your sins will always find you out! I guess I'll never be able to keep a good job for long. Somebody will always put it round that I was a thief once, and that my parents are still in prison.'

'Gladys—the person who wrote that letter and threatens to tell about you, is far, far wickeder than you've *ever* been!' said Fatty earnestly. 'It's a shame!'

'There was another girl in the Home with me,' said Gladys. 'She's with old Miss Garnet at Lacky Cottage in Peterswood. Well, she's had one of them letters too—without any name at the bottom. But she doesn't mind as much as I do. She didn't give way like I did. But she met me and told me, that's how I know. She didn't tell nobody but me. And she don't know either who wrote the letters.

'Did you tell Mr. Goon that?' asked Fatty.

'Oh yes,' said Gladys. 'And he went to see Molly straight-away. He says he'll soon get to the bottom of it, and find out the mischief-maker. But it seems to me that the mischief is done now. I'll never be able to face people in Peterswood again. I'll always be afraid they know about me.'

'Gladys, where is that letter?' said Fatty. 'Wll you show it to me? It might be a most important clue.'

Gladys rummaged in her bag. Then she looked up. 'No good me looking for it!' she said. 'I've given it to Mr. Goon, of course! He came to fetch it this morning. He's got Molly's letter too. He reckons he'll be able to tell quite a lot from the writing and all!'

'Blow!' said Fatty, in deep disappointment. 'There's our one and only clue gone!'

THE children sat and talked to Gladys for a little while longer. They were so disappointed about the letter being given to Mr.Goon that she felt quite sorry for them.'

'I'll get it back from him, and Molly's letter too,' she promised. 'And I'll show you them both. I'll be going down to see Molly this evening, when it's dark and no one will see me—and I'll pop into Mr. Goon's, say I want to borrow the letters, and I'll lend them to you for a little while.'

'Oh thanks!' said Fatty, cheering up. 'That'll be splendid. Well, now we'd better be going. We've got our lunch with us and it's getting a bit late-ish. You haven't put that dinner on yet Gladys, either?'

'Oh lawks, nor I have!' said Gladys, and began to look very flustered. 'I've been that upset I can't think of a thing!'

'You'll be passing my door on your way to Molly's to-night,' said Fatty. 'Could you pop the letters in at my letter-box, and call for them on your way back?'

'Yes, I'll do that,' said Gladys. 'Thank you for all your kindness. You've made me feel better already.'

The children went off. 'A nice girl, but not very bright,' said Fatty, as they cycled away. 'What a mean trick to play on her—trying to make her lose her job and get all upset like that! I wonder who in the world it is? I bet it's some one who knows the Home Gladys went to, and has heard about her there. My goodness, I'm hungry!'

'We've had quite and exciting morning,' said Larry. 'It's a pity we couldn't see that letter though.'

'Never mind—we'll see it is this evening—if old Clear-Orf will let Gladys have it!' said Fatty. 'Which I very much doubt. He'll suspect she's going to show it to us!'

'We'll all come round to you after tea,' said Larry. 'And we'll wait for the letters to come. I think you'd better wait about by the front gate, Fatty—just in case somebody else takes them out of the letter-box instead of you.'

So, when it was dark, Fatty skulked about by the front gate, scaring his mother considerably when she came home from an outing.

'Good gracious, Fatty! Must you hide in the shadows there?' she said. 'You gave me an awful fright. Go in at once.'

'Sorry, Mother,' said Fatty, and went meekly in at the front door with his mother—and straight out of the garden door, back to the front gate at once! Just in time too, for a shadowy figure leaned over the gate and said breathlessly: 'Is that Master Frederick? Here's the letters. Mr. Goon was out, so I went in and waited. He didn't come, so I took them, and here they are.'

Gladys pushed a packet into Fatty's hands and hurried off. Fatty gave a low whistle. Gladys hadn't waited for permission to take the letters! She had reckoned they were hers and Molly's and had just taken them, What would Mr. Goon say to that? He wouldn't be at all pleased with Gladys—especially when he knew she had

Gladys pushed the letter into Fatty's hand

handed them to him, Fatty! Fatty knew perfectly well that Mr. Goon would get it all out of poor Gladys.

He slipped indoors and told the others what had happened. 'Think I'd better try and put the letters back without old Clear-Orf knowing they've gone,' he said. 'If I don't Gladys will get into trouble. But first of all, we'll examine them!'

'I suppose it's all right to?' said Larry doubtfully.

'Well—I don't see that it matters, seeing that Gladys had given us her permission,' said Fatty. He looked at the little package.

'Golly!' he said. 'There are more than two letters here! Look—here's a post-card—an anonymous one to Mr. Lucas, Gardener, Acacia Lodge, Peterswood—and do you know what it says?'

'What?' cried every one.

'Why, it says: "WHO LOST HIS JOB THROUGH SELLING HIS MASTER'S FRUIT?' said Fatty, in disgust. 'Gracious! Fancy sending a *card* with that on—to poor old Lucas too, who must be over seventy!'

'So other people have had these beastly things as well as Gladys and Molly!' said Larry. 'Let's squint at the writing, Fatty.'

'It's all the same,' said Fatty. 'All done in capital letters, look—and all to people in Peterswood. There are five of them—four letters and a card. How disgusting!'

Larry was examining the envelopes. They were all the same, square and white, and the paper used was cheap. 'Look,' said Larry, 'they've all been sent from Sheepsale—that little market-town we've sometimes been to. Does the mean it's somebody who lives there?'

'Not necessarily,' said Fatty. 'No, I reckon it's somebody who lives in Peterswood all right, because only a Peterswood person would know the people written to. What exactly does the post-mark say?'

'It says, "Sheepsale, 11.45 .am. April 3rd," said Daisy.

'That was Monday,' said Fatty. 'What do the other post-marks say?'

'They're all different dates,' said Daisy. 'All of them except Gladys's one are posted in March—but all from Sheepsale.'

Fatty made a note of the dates and then took a small pocket calendar out. He looked up the dates and whistled.

'Here's a funny thing,' he said. 'They're all a Monday! See—that one's a Monday—and so is that—and that—and that. Whoever posted them must have written them on the Sunday, and posted them on Monday. Now—if the person lives in Peterswood, how can he get to Sheepsale to post them in time for the morning post on a Monday? There's no railway to Sheepsale. Only a bus that doesn't go very often.'

'It's market-day on Mondays at Sheepsale,' said Pip, remembering. 'There's an early bus that goes then, to catch the market. Wait a bit—we can look it up. Where's a bus time-table?'

As usual, Fatty had one in his pocket. He looked up the Sheepsale bus.

'Yes—here we are,' he said. 'There's a bus that goes to Sheepsale from Peterswood each Monday—at a quarter-past ten—reaching there at one minute past eleven. There you are—I bet our letter-writing friend leaves

Peterswood with a nasty letter in his pocket, catches the bus, gets out at Sheepsale, posts the letter—and then gets on with whatever business he has to do there!'

It all sounded extremely likely, but somehow Larry thought it was *too* likely. 'Couldn't the person go on a bike?' he said.

'Well—he *could*—but think of that awful hill up to Sheepsale,' said Fatty. 'Nobody in their senses would bike there when a bus goes.'

'No—I suppose not,' said Larry. 'Well—I don't see that all this gets us much farther, Fatty. All we've found out is that more people than Gladys and Molly have had there letters—and that they all come from Sheepsale and posted at or before 11.45—and that possibly the letter-writer may catch the 10.15 bus from Peterswood.'

'*All* we've found out!' said Fatty. 'Gosh, I think we've discovered an enormous lot. Don't you realize that we're really on the track now—the track of this beastly letter-writer. Why, if we want to, we can go and see him—or her—on Monday morning!'

The others stared at Fatty, puzzled.

'We've only got to catch that 10.15 bus!' said Fatty. "See? The letter-writer is sure to be on it. Can't we discover who it is just by looking at their faces? I bet *I* can!'

'Oh, Fatty!' said Bets, full of admiration . 'Of course—we'll catch that bus. But, oh dear, *I* should never be able to tell the right person, never. Will you really be able to spot who it is?'

'Well, I'll have a jolly good try,' said Fatty. 'And now I'd better take these letters back, I think. But first of

all I want to make a tracing of some of these sentences—
especially words like "PETERSWOOD" that occur in each
address—in case I come across somebody who prints their
words in just that way.'

'People don't print words, though—they write them,'
said Daisy. But Fatty took no notice. He carefully traced
a few of the words, one of them being 'PETERS-
WOOD'. He put the slip into his wallet. Then he snapped
the bit of elastic round the package and stood up.

'How are you going to get the letters back without
being seen?' asked Larry.

'Don't know yet,' said Fatty, with a grin. 'Just chance
my luck, I think. Wait about for Gladys, will you, and
tell her I didn't approve of her taking the letters like that
in case Mr. Goon was angry with her—amd tell her I'm
returning him the letters, and hope he won't know she
took them at all.'

'Right,' said Larry. Fatty was about to go when he
turned and came back. 'I've an idea I'd better pop on
my telegraph-boy's uniform,' he said. 'Just in case old
Goon spots me. I don't want him to know *I'm* returning
his letters!'

It wasn't long before Fatty was wearing his disguise,
complete with freckles, red eyebrows and hair. He set
this telegraph-boy's cap on his head.

'So long!' he said, and disappeared. He padded off
to Mr. Goon's, and soon saw, by the darkness of his
parlour, that he was not yet back. So he waited about,
until he remembered that there was a darts match at the
local inn, and guessed Mr. Goon would be there, throw-
ing a dart or two.

His guess was right. Mr. Goon walked out of the inn in about ten minutes' time, feeling delighted with himself because he had come out second in the match. Fatty padded behind him for a little way, then ran across the road, got in front of Mr. Goon, came across again at a corner, walked towards the policeman and bumped violently into him.

'Hey!' said the policeman, all his breath knocked out of him. 'Hey! Look where you're going now.' He flashed his torch and saw the red-handed telegraph-boy.

'Sorry, sir, I do beg your pardon,' said Fatty earnestly. 'Have I hurt you? Always seem to be damaging you, don't I, sir? Sorry, sir.'

Mr. Goon set his helmet straight. Fatty's apologies soothed him. 'All right, my boy, all right,' he said.

'Good-night, sir, thank you, sir,' said Fatty and disappeared. But he hadn't gone more than three steps before he came running back again, holding out a package.

'Oh, Mr. Goon, Sir, did you drop these, sir? Or has somebody else dropped them?'

Mr. Goon stared at the package and his eyes bulged. 'Them letters!' he said. 'I didn't take them out with me, that I do know!'

'I expect they belong to somebody else then,' said Fatty. 'I'll inquire.'

'Hey, no you don't!' said Mr. Goon, making a grab at the package. 'They're my property. I must have brought them out unbeknowing-like. Dropped them when you bumped into me, shouldn't wonder. Good thing you found them, young man. They're valuable evidence, they are. Property of the Law.'

'I hope you won't drop them again, then, sir,' said Fatty earnestly. 'Good-night, sir.'

He vanished. Mr. Goon went home in a thoughtful frame of mind, pondering how he could possibly have taken out the package of letters and dropped them. He felt sure he *hadn't* taken them out—but if not, how could he have dropped them?

'Me memory's going,' he said mournfully. 'It's a mercy one of them kids didn't pick them letters up. I won't let that there Frederick Trotteville set eyes on them. Not if I know it!'

10 ON THE BUS TO SHEEPSALE

THERE was nothing more to be done until Monday morning, The children felt impatient, but they couldn't hurry the coming of Monday, or of the bus either.

Fatty had entered a few notes under his heading of Clues. He had put down all about the anonymous letters, and the post-marks, and had also pinned to the page the tracings he had made of the printing capital letters.

'I will now write up the case as far as we've gone with it,' he said. 'That's what the police do—and all good detectives too, as far as I can see. Sort of clears your mind, you see. Sometimes you get awfully, good ideas when you read what you've written.

Every one read what Fatty wrote, and they thought it was excellent. But infortunately nobody had any good ideas after reading it. Still, the bus passengers to Sheepsale might provide further clues.

The five children couldn't help feeling rather excited on Monday morning. Larry and Daisy got rather a shock when their mother said she wanted them to go shopping for her—but when she heard that they were going to Sheepsale market she said they could buy the things for her there. So that was all right.

They met at the bus stopping-place ten minutes before the bus went, in case Fatty had any last-minute instructions for them. He had !

'Look and see where the passengers are sitting when the bus comes up,' he said. 'And each of you sit beside one if you can, and begin to talk to him or her. You can find out a lot that way.'

Bets looked alarmed. 'But I shan't know what to say !' she said.

'Don't be silly,' said Pip. 'You can always open the conversation by saying, "Isn't that a remarkably clever-looking boy over there?" and point to Fatty. That's enough to get any one talking.'

They all laughted. 'It's all right, Bets,' said Fatty. 'You can always say something simple, like "Can you tell me the time, please?" Or, "What is this village we're passing now?" It's easy to make people talk if you ask them to *tell* you something.'

'Any other instructions, Sherlock Holmes?' said Pip.

'Yes—and this is most important,' said Fatty. 'We must watch carefully whether anybody posts a letter in Sheepsale—because if only one of the passengers does, that's a pretty good pointer, isn't it ? The post-office is by the bus-stop there, so we can easily spot if any one catches the 11.45 post. We can hang around and see if any of the bus passengers posts a letter before that time, supposing they don't go to the letter-box immediately. That's a most important point.'

'Here comes the bus,' said Bets in excitement. 'And look—there are quite a lot of people in it !'

'Five !' said Larry. 'One for each of us. Oh gosh ! One of them is old Clear-Orf ! '

'Blow !' said Fatty. 'So it is. Now whatever is he doing on the bus this morning? Has he got the same idea as we have, I wonder? If so, he's brainier than I thought. Daisy, you sit by him. He'll have a blue fit if I do and I know Buster will try to nibble his ankles all the time.'

Daisy was not at all anxious to sit by Mr. Goon, but there was no time to argue. The bus stopped. The five children and Buster got in. Buster gave a yelp of joy when he smelt the policeman. Mr. Goon looked round in astonishment and annoyance.

'Gah !' he said, in tones of deep disgust. 'You again ! Now, what you doing on this bus to-day ! Everywhere I go there's you children traipsing along !'

'We're going to Sheepsale markert, Mr. Goon,' said Daisy politely, sitting beside him. 'I hope you don't mind. Are you going there too?'

'That's *my* business,' said Mr. Goon, keeping a watchful eye on Buster, who was trying to reach his ankles, straining at his lead. 'What the Law does is no concern of yours.'

Daisy wondered for a wild moment if Mr. Goon could possibly be the anonymous letter-writter. After all, he knew the histories of every one in the village. It was his business to. Then she knew it was mad idea. But what a nuisance if Mr. Goon was on the same track as they were—sizing up the people in the bus, and going to watch for the one who posted the letter to catch the 11.45 post.

Daisy glanced round at the other people in the bus. A Find-Outer was by each. Daisy knew two of the people there. One was Miss Trimble who was companion to Lady Candling, Pip's next-door neighbour. Larry was sitting by her. Daisy felt certain Miss Trimble—or Tremble as the children called her, could have nothing to do with the case. She was far too timid and nervous.

Then there was fat little Mrs. Jolly from the sweet-shop, kindness itself. No, it couldn't possibly be her ! Why, every one loved her, and she was exactly like her name. She was kind and generous to every one, and she nodded and smiled at Daisy as she caught her eye. Daisy was certain that before the trip was ended she would be handing sweets out to all the children !

Well, that was three out of the five passengers ! That only left two possible ones. One was a thin, dark, sour-faced man, huddled up over a newspaper, with a pasty complexion, and a curious habit of twitching his nose like a rabbit every now and again. This fascinated Bets, who kept watching him.

The other possible person was a yound girl about eighteen, carrying sketching things. She had a sweet, open face, and very pretty curly hair. Daisy felt abso-lutely certain that she knew nothing what-ever about the letters.

'It must be that sour-faced man with the twitching nose,'

said Daisy to herself. She had nothing much to do because it was no use tackling Mr. Goon and talking to him. It was plain that he could not be the writer of the letters. So she watched the others getting to work, and listened with much interest, though the rattling of the bus made her miss a little of the conversation.

'Good morning, Miss Trimble,' Daisy heared Larry say politely. 'I haven't seen you for some time. Are you going to the market too? We thought we'd like to go to-day.'

'Oh, it's a pretty sight,' said Miss Trimble, setting her glasses firmly on her nose. They were always falling off, for they were pince-nez, with no side-pieces to hold them behind her ears. Bets loved to count how many times they fell off. What with watching the man with the twitching nose and Miss Timble's glasses, Bets quite forgot to talk to Mrs. Jolly, who was taking up most of the seat she and Bets was sitting on.

'Have you often been to Sheepsale market?' asked Larry.

'No, not very often,' said Miss Trimble. 'How is your dear mother, Laurence?'

'She's quite well,' said Larry. 'Er—how is *your* mother, Miss Tremble? I remember seeing her once next door.'

'Ah, my dear mother isn't too well,' said Miss Trimble. 'And if you don't mind, Laurence dear, my name is *Trimble,* not Tremble. I think I have told you that before,'

'Sorry. I keep forgetting,' said Larry. 'Er—does your mother live at Sheepsale, Miss Trem—er Trimble? Do you often go and see her?'

'She lives just outside Sheepsale,' said Miss Trimble, pleased at Larry's interest in her mother. 'Dear Lady Candling lets me go every Monday to see her, you know—such a help. I do all the old lady's shopping for the week then.'

'Do you always catch this bus?' asked Larry, wondering if by any conceivable chance Miss Trimble could be the wicked letter-writer.

'If I can,' said Miss Trimble. 'The next one is not till after lunch you know.'

Larry turned and winked at Fatty.. He didn't think that Miss Trimble was the guilty person, but at any rate she must be down as a suspect. But her next words made him change his mind completely.

'It was such a nuisance,' said Miss Trimble. 'I lost the bus last week, and wasted half my day!'

Well! That put Miss Trimble right out of the question, because certainly the letter-writer had posted the letter to poor Gladys the Monday before—and if Miss Trimble had missed the bus, she couldn't have been in Sheepsale at the right time for posting!

Larry decided that he couldn't get any more out of Miss Trimble that would be any use and looked out of the window. Bets seemed to be getting on well with Mrs. Jolly now. He couldn't hear what she was saying, but he could see that she was busy chattering.

Bets was getting on like a house on fire! Mrs. Jolly greeted her warmly and asked after her mother and father, and how the garden was, and had they still got that kitchen cat that was such a good hunter. And Bets answered all her questions, keeping an interested eye on Miss Trimble's glasses and on the sour-faced man's twitching nose.

It was not until she saw how earnestly Fatty was trying to make the sour-faced man talk to him that she suddenly realized that she too ought to find out a few things from Mrs. Jolly. Whether, for instance, she always caught this bus!

'Are you going to the market, Mrs. Jolly?' she asked.

'Yes, that I am!' said Mrs. Jolly. 'I always but my butter and eggs from my sister there. You should go to her stall too, Miss Bets, and tell her you know me. She'll give you over-weight in butter then and maybe a brown egg for yourself!'

'She sounds awfully kind—just like you' said Bets.

Mrs. Jolly was pleased and laughed her hearty laugh. 'Oh, you've got a soft tongue, haven't you?' she said. Bets was surprised. She thought all tongues must surely be soft.

She looked at Mrs. Jolly, and decided not to ask her any more questions about going to Sheepsale every Monday because nobody, nobody with such kind eyes, such a lovely smile, such a nice apple-cheeked face could possibly write an unkind letter! Bets felt absolutely certain of it. Mrs. Jolly began to fumble in her bag.

'Now where did I put those humbugs?' she said. 'Ah, here they are? Do you like humbugs, Miss Bets? Well, you help yourself, and we'll pass them over to the others as well.'

Pip was sitting by the young girl. He found it easy to talk to her..

'What are you going to paint?' he asked.

'I'm painting Sheepsale market,' she answered. 'I go every Monday. It's such a jolly market—small and friendly and very picturesque, set on the top of the hill, with that lovely country all round. I love it.'

'Do you always catch the same bus?' asked Pip.

'I have to,' she said. 'The market's in the morning, you know. I know it by heart now—where the hens and ducks are, and the sheep, and the butter-stalls and the eggs and everything!'

'I bet you don't know where the post-office is!' said Pip quickly.

The girl laughed and thought. 'Well, no, I don't!' she said. 'I've never had to go there and so I've never noticed. But if you want it, any one would tell you. There can't be much of a post-office at Sheepsale though. It's only a small place. Just a market really.'

Pip felt pleased. If this girl didn't know where the post-office was, she could never have posted a letter there. Good. That ruled her out. Pip felt very clever. Anyway, he was certain that such a nice girl wouldn't write horrid letters.

He looked round at the others, feeling that his task was done. He felt sorry for Daisy, sitting next to the surly Mr. Goon. He wondered how Fatty was getting on.

He wasn't getting on at all well! Poor Fatty—he had chosen a very difficult passenger to talk to.

THE sour-faced man appeared to be very deep indeed in his paper, which seemed to Fatty to be all about horses and dogs.

Buster sniffed at the man's ankles and didn't seem to like the smell of them at all. He gave a disgusted snort and strained away towards where Mr. Goon sat, a few seats in fornt.

'Er—I hope my dog doesn't worry you, sir,' said Fatty.

The man took no notice. 'Must be deaf,' thought Fatty and raised his voice considerably.

'I hope my DOG doesn't WORRY you, sir,' he said. The man looked up and scowled.

'Don't shout at me. I'm not deaf,' he said.

Fatty didn't like to ask again if Buster worried him. He cast about for something interesting to say.

'Er—horses and dogs are very interesting aren't they?' he said. The man took no notice. Fatty debated whether to raise his voice or not. He decided not.

'I said, horses and dogs are very interesting, aren't they?' he repeated.

Depends,' said the man, and went on reading.

That wasn't much help in a conversation, Fatty thought gloomily. The others were jolly lucky to have got such easy people to tackle. But still—of all the passengers in the bus, this man looked by far the most likely to be the letter-writer—sour-faced, scowling, cruel-mouthed! Fatty racked his brains and tried again.

'Er—could you tell me the time?' he said, rather feebly. There was no reply. This was getting boring! Fatty couldn't help feeling annoyed too. There was no need to be so rude, he thought!

'Could you tell me the time?' he repeated.

'I could, but I'm not going to, seeing that you've got a wrist-watch yourself,' said the man. Fatty could have kicked himself.

'You're not being much of a detective this morning!' he told himself. 'Buck up, Frederick Algernon Trotteville, and look sharp about it!'

'Oh—look at that aeroplane!' said Fatty, seeing a plane swoop down rather low. 'Do you know what it is, sir?'

'Flying Fortress,' said the man, without even looking up. As the aeroplane had only two engines and not four, this was quite wrong and Fatty knew it. He looked at his fellow passenger in despair. How could he ever get anything out of him?'

'I'm going to Sheepsale market,' he said. 'Are you, sir?'

There was no answer. Fatty wished Buster would bite the man's ankles. 'Do you know if this is Buckle Village we're passing?' asked Fatty, as they passed through a pretty little village. The man put down his paper and glared at Fatty angrily.

'I'm a stranger here,' he said. 'I know nothing about Buckle or Sheepsale or its market! I'm just going there to be picked up by my brother, to go on some where else—and all I can say is that the further I get away form chatterboxes like you, the better I shall like it!'

As this was all said very loudly, most of the people in the bus heard it. Mr. Goon chuckled heartily.

'Ah, I've had some of him too!' he called. 'Proper pest, I reckon he is.'

'Go and sit somewhere else and take your smelly dog with you,' said the sour-faced man, pleased to find that somebody else agreed with his opinion of poor Fatty.

So Fatty, red in the face, and certain that he would not be able to get anything more out of the annoyed man, got up and went right to the front of the bus, where nobody was sitting. Bets was sorry for him and she left Mrs. Jolly and joined him.

Larry, Pip and Daisy came across too, and they talked together in low voices.

'I can't see that it can be any one here,' said Fatty, when he had heard all that the others had to say. 'It's obviously not old Clear-Orf—and we can rule out Miss Tremble and Mrs. Jolly surely. And I agree with Pip that the artist girl isn't very likely either, especially as she doesn't even know where the post-office is. And my man said he was a stranger here, so it doesn't look as if he could be the one. A stranger wouldn't know any of the Peterswood people.'

'Does he come on this bus every Monday?' asked Pip, in a low voice.

'I didn't get as far as asking him that,' said Fatty gloomily. 'Either he wouldn't answer, or he just snapped. He was hopeless. It doesn't look really as if any of the people here could have posted those letters.'

'Look—there's somebody waiting at the next bus-stop!' said Bets suddenly. 'At least—it isn't a bus-stop—it's just somebody waving to the bus to stop it for himself. That must be the person we want, if there's nobody else.'

'Perhaps it is,' said Fatty hopefully, and they all waited to see who came in.

But it was the vicar of Buckle! The children knew him quite well because he sometimes came to talk to them in their own church at Peterswood. He was a jolly, burly man and they liked him.

'Can't be him!' said Fatty, disappointed. 'Can't possibly. Blow! We're not a bit further on.'

'Never mind—perhaps one of them will post a letter when they get out of the bus,' said Pip. 'We'll hope for that. Maybe your sour-faced man will, Fatty. He looks the most likely of the lot. He may be telling lies when he says he is a stranger.'

The vicar talked to every one in the bus in his cheerful booming voice. The thin huddled man took no notice, and as the Vicar did not greet him, the children felt sure that he did not know him. So perhaps he *was* a stranger after all?

'Soon be at Sheepsale now,' said Fatty. Golly, isn't this a steep pull-up? They say it wanted eight horses to pull the coach up in the old days before motor-buses.'

The bus stopped under some big trees in Sheepsale. A babel of baaing, mooing, clucking and quacking came to every one's ears. The market was in full swing!

'Quick—hop out first!' said Fatty to the others. 'Stand by the post-office—and keep a close watch.'

The children hurried off. Miss Trimble nodded to

them and walked away down a little lane. The Find-Outers spotted the post-office at once and went over to it. Fatty produced a letter, and began to stamp it carefully.

'Don't want Goon to wonder why we're all standing about here,' he murmured to the others. 'May as well post this letter.'

Mrs. Jolly went off to the market to find her sister. The children watched her go.

'Well, neither Miss Trimble nor Mrs. Jolly have posted letters,' said Fatty. 'That lets those two out. Ah— here comes the artist girl.'

The girl smiled at them and went on. Then she suddenly turned back. 'I see you've found the post-office!' she called. 'I'm so glad! How silly of me never to have noticed it when I pass it every single Monday. But that's just like me!'

'She's not the one, either,' said Pip, as she disappeared in the direction of the market. 'I didn't think she was. She was too nice.'

The vicar disappeared too, without coming in their direction at all. Now only Mr. Goon and the sour-faced man were left. Mr. Goon stared at Fatty, and Fatty raised his eyebrows and smiled sweetly.

'Anything I can do for you, Mr. Goon?'

'What you hanging about here for?' said the policeman. 'Funny thing I can't seem to get rid of you children. Always hanging on my tail, you are.'

'We were thinking the same thing about you too,' said Fatty. He watched the sour-faced man, who was standing nearby at the kerb, still reading his paper about dogs and horses. Fatty wondered if he wanted to post a letter, but was waiting till the children and Mr. Goon had gone. Or was he *really* waiting for his brother, as he had said?

'There's the sweet-shop over the road,' said Fatty, in a low voice, popping his letter into the post-box. 'Let's go over there and buy something. We can keep a watch on the post-box all the time. Then if dear old Clear-Orf or the sour-faced fellow are bursting to post letters, they can do it without feeling that we are watching!'

So they all crossed to the sweet-shop and went in. Larry and Daisy started an argument about whether to buy peppermints or toffees, and Fatty watched the post-office carefully through the glass door. He could see, but could not be seen, for it was dark in the little shop.

The sour-faced man folded up his paper and looked up and down the village street. Mr. Goon disappeared into a tobacco shop. Fatty watched breathlessly. There was no one about in the street now—would that man quickly slip a letter into the post-box?

A car drove up. The driver called out a greeting, and the sour-faced man replied. He opened the door and got in beside the driver. Then they drove off quickly. Fatty gave such a heavy sigh that the others looked round.

'He didn't post a letter,' said Fatty. 'He was telling the truth. Somebody picked him up in a car. Blow! Bother! Dash!'

'Well, even if he *had* posted a letter, I don't see that we could have collared him,' said Pip. 'We didn't know his name or anything about him. But I say—it's pretty peculiar, isn't it—not a single one of the passengers posted a letter—and yet one is always posted every single

Monday!'

'Well—we'll just wait till 11.45 when the postman comes to collet the letters,' said Fatty. 'In case one of the passengers come back. Ah, there goes Goon, off to the market. I suppose he's buying butter and cream to make himself a bit fatter!'

The children waited patiently by the post-office till the postman came and took out the letters. Nobody came to post any. It was most disappointing.

'We're just where we were!' said Fatty gloomily. 'Sickening, isn't it? I don't think we're such good detectives as we hoped we were! You go off to the market. I want to have a good think. I may get a much better idea soon!'

So off to Sheepsale market went the others, leaving poor Fatty behind, looking extremely gloomy.

12   A LOVELY DAY

THE children had a really lovely time at the market. They loved every minute of it. It was such a noisy, lively, friendly place, the birds and animals were so excited, the market-folk so good-humoured and talkative.

They found Mrs. Jolly's sister, and she insisted on giving each of them a large brown egg, and a small pat of her golden home-made butter for their breakfast. Bets was simply delighted. She always loved an unexpected present more than any other.

'Oh *thank* you!' she said. 'You *are* kind—just exactly

like Mrs. Jolly. She gives us sweets. Is your name Jolly, too?'

'No. I'm Mrs. Bunn,' said Mrs. Jolly's sister and Bets very nearly said, 'Oh, that's *just* the right name for you!' but stopped herself in time. For Mrs. Bunn was exactly like her name—big and round, and soft and warm, with eyes like black-currants.

'Let's go and find Fatty and tell him to come and see the market,' said Bets. 'I don't like to think of him glooming by himself. We're stuck over this case, and I don't believe even Fatty can unstick us.'

'There's the artist girl, look!' said Pip. And there she was, in the middle of the market, painting hard, gazing at all the animals and birds around her in delight. The children went and looked at her picture and thought it was very good indeed.

Bets went to find Fatty. He was sitting on a bench in the village street, lost in thought. Bets looked at him in admiration. She could quite will imagine him grown-up, solving deep mysteries that nobody else could. She went up to him and made him jump.

'Oh, Fatty, sorry! Did I make you jump? Do come and see the market. It's marvellous.'

'I haven't quite finished my pondering yet,' said Fatty. Perhaps if I talk to you , Bets, I might see things a little more clearly.

Bets was thrilled and proud. 'Oh yes, *do* talk to me Flatty. I'll listen and not say a word.'

'Oh, you can talk too,' said Fatty. 'You're a very sensible little person, I think. I haven't forgotten how you guessed that telegraph-boy was me, just because you happened to see Buster staring up at me adoringly.'

Buster looked up at the mention of his name. He was looking gloomy, because he was still on the lead. He badly wanted to go off to the market, because the smells that came from it were too exciting for words. He wagged his tail feebly.

'Buster looks as if he's pondering too,' said Bets. Fatty took no notice. He was looking off into the distance, deep in thought. Bets decided not to disturb him. He could talk to her when he wanted to. She began to practise twitching her nose just as she had seen the sour-faced man do. Buster watched her.

Fatty suddenly noticed it too and stared. 'Whatever's the matter with your nose?' he said.

'I'm only just twitching it like that man did,' said Bets. 'Talk to me, Fatty.'

'Well, I'm trying to work out what's best to do next,' said Fatty. 'Now—every Monday for some weeks past somebody has posted a letter to catch the 11.45 post here in Sheepsale—and each of those letters has gone to people in Peterswood. Well, if you remember, I said that that looked as if somebody living in Peterswood, who knew those people and possibly their histories, must have posted them.'

'Yes, that's right,' said Bets.

'And we worked out that the letter-writer probably caught that bus on a Monday and posted the letter on getting out,' said Fatty. 'So we caught the same bus, but we haven't found any one we could *really* suspect— though mind you every one of those bus passengers must go down on out list of Suspects—and we didn't catch any one posting a letter either.'

'You're not going to put Clear-Orf or the vicar down on the list, are you?' said Bets, astonished.

'Every single person is being put there,' said Fatty firmly. 'We can easily cross them out if we think we should—but they've all got to go down.'

'I dare say Clear-Orf has put *us* all down on *his* list of Suspects too then,' said Bets unexpectedly. 'I expect he was on that bus for the same reason as we were—to have a look at the passengers and watch who posted a letter.'

Fatty stared at Bets. Then he burst out into such a hearty laugh that Bets was startled. 'Have I said something funny?' she asked.

'No, Bets. But don't you realize which of the passengers posted a letter?' said Fatty, grinning.

'Nobody did,' said Bets. 'Well—expect you, of course!'

'Yes—me!' said Fatty. 'And it's going to make old Goon scratch his head hard when he thinks that of all his precious Suspects only one posted a letter—and that was his pet aversion, Frederick Trotteville!'

Bets laughed too. 'That's funny!' she said. 'But, Fatty, nobody could possibly think *you* would write horrid letters like that!'

'Old Clear-Orf would believe I'd stolen the Crown Jewels, if there was any suspicion of it,' He'd think me capable of anything. Golly—he must be in a state, wondering who's going to get that letter to-morrow morning!'

'And nobody *will* get a letter!' said Bets. 'Because one hasn't been posted. It will be the first Monday that is missed for six weeks. I wonder why?'

'So do I,' said Fatty. 'Of course—if one *does* arrive—it will mean that the writer lives in Sheepsale after all, and has just posted the letter any time this morning, before the bus came up. Then we shall be properly stuck. We can't watch all the inhabitants of Sheepsale posting letters!'

'Perhaps whoever comes up on the bus to post the letters each Monday didn't come to-day for some reason,' said Bets.

'That's an idea,' said Fatty. 'When we go back on the bus we'll ask the conductor if he always has his regular passengers each Monday, and see if any didn't go this morning. We could make inquiries about them too—see if they've got any spite against Gladys or Molly or the others, and so on.'

'When's the next bus back?' asked Bets. 'I wish we could stay here for the day, Fatty. You'd love the market. But we haven't got our lunch with us.'

'We could have it in that little shop over there,' said Fatty, pointing. 'Look—it says, 'Light Lunches.' That probably means eggs and bread, and butter and cake. How would you like that?'

'Oh, it would be *lovely*,' said Bets. 'I wish we could stay here for the day, Fatty. You'd love the market. But Mother would be anxious if we didn't come back.'

'I'll do a spot of phoning,' said Fatty, who never minded doing things of that sort. Bets thought how like a grown-up he was, always deciding things, and, what was more, always seeming to have plenty of money to pay for everything!

Fatty disappeared into the post-office and went into the telephone box. He made three calls very quickly and came out.

'It's all right,' he said. 'I phoned up your mother and Larry's mother and mine—and they all said, 'Good riddance to you for the day!'

'They didn't, Fatty!' said Bets, who simply couldn't imagine her mother saying any such thing.

'Well—not exactly those words,' grinned Fatty. 'But I could tell they weren't sorry to be rid of us for the day. I don't think my mother, for instance, liked that new game of ours very much.'

'I shouldn't think she did, really,' said Bets, remembering the yowling and groaning and rolling over and over that went with Fatty's new game. 'Let's go and tell the others we can stay here for lunch. Won't they be thrilled!'

They were. 'Good old Fatty!' said Larry. 'It's a treat to be up here on a day like this, among all the forming folk and their creatures. What's the time? I'm getting jolly hungry.'

'It's a quarter to one,' said Fatty. 'I vote we go and have some lunch now. Come on. It looks a nice little place like a dairy and cake shop mixed.'

It *was* a nice little place—shining and spotless, with a plump woman in a vast white apron to serve them and beam at them.

Yes, she could do two boiled eggs a piece and some plates of bread and butter, and some of her own bottled gooseberries if they liked, with a jug of cream. And she'd made some new buns, would they like some?

'This is just the kind of meal I like,' said Bets, as the eggs arrived, all brown and smooth and warm. 'I like it much better than meat. Oh—is that strawberry jam, how lovely!'

'I thought you might like some with the bread and butter, after you've had your eggs,' said the plump woman, smiling at them all. 'They're my own growing, the strawberries.'

'I think,' said Daisy, battering with her spoon at her egg, 'I think that there can't be any thing nicer than to keep your own hens and ducks, and grow your own fruit and vegetables, and do your own bottling, and pickling, and jamming. When I'm grown-up I'm not going to get a job in an office and write dreary letters, or things like that —I'm going to keep a little house and have my own birds and animals and make all kinds of delicious food like this!'

'In that case,' said Larry, 'I shall come and live with you, Daisy—especially if you make jam like this!'

'I'll come too,' said both Fatty and Pip at once.

'Oh—wouldn't it be lovely if we could *all* live together, and have lovely meals like this, and solve mysteries for the rest of our lives!' said Bets fervently.

Everybody laughed. Bets always took things they said so seriously.

'Well, I can't say we've made much headway at solving *this* one!' said Fatty, beginning his second egg. 'All right, Buster, old fellow, we'll get you a meal too when we've finished. Be patient!'

Fatty paid the smiling woman for the meal when they

had finished. The others wanted to pay their share, but hadn't enough money. 'We'll take it out of our money-boxes when we get home,' said Larry. 'And give it to you, Fatty.'

'That's all right,' said Fatty. 'Now let's go and watch them clearing up the market. Then we'd better inquire about our bus.'

They spent a lovely time watching the market folk packing up their unsold goods, taking away the birds and animals bought and sold, talking, laughing, and clapping one another on the back. Mrs. Jolly was there, talking to her sister, and she called to them.

'Don't you miss that bus back now! There's only two more to-day, and the last one goes too late for you!'

'Golly! We forgot to look up the bus-time,' said Fatty, and ran to a bus time-table to look. 'We've only got three minutes!' he said. 'Come on, we must run for it!'

They caught the bus with about half a minute to spare. But to Fatty's deep disappointment the driver and conductor were different. Apparently the morning and afternoon buses were manned by different men.

'Blow!' said Fatty, sitting down at the front. 'I call this a real waste of a day!'

'Oh *Fatty*—how can you say that?' said Daisy, who had enjoyed every single minute of it. 'Why, it's been the nicest day we've had these hols!'

'I daresay,' said Fatty. 'But of you remember, we came up here to try and get a bit further forward in our Mystery—and all we've done is to have a jolly good time, and not find out anything at all. A good day for five children—but a poor day for the Find-Outers–and Dog !'

13　ANOTHER OF THOSE LETTERS

NEXT day the children felt rather full after their exciting time at the market. They met in Pip's playroom, and Fatty seemed rather gloomy.

'I wish we could find out if any one has had an anonymous letter *this* Tuesday,' he said. 'But I don't see how we can. Old Clear-Orf is in a much better position than we are—such a thing would probably be reported to him at once !'

'Well—never mind about the letters to-day,' said Pip. 'My mother's out—so if you want to play that woo-hoo-colly-wobbles game, we can.'

'Won't Mrs. Moon object ?' asked Fatty.

'I shouldn't think she'd hear, away down in the kitchen,' said Pip. 'Anyway, we don't need to bother about her!'

They were just beginning their extremely hilarious game, when a knock came at the playroom door and Mrs. Moon stuck her head in. The children looked at her, expecting a complaint.

But she hadn't come to complain. 'Master Philip, I've got to run down to the shops,' she said. 'The butcher hasn't sent me my kidneys this morning. Will you answer the telephone whilst I'm gone, and listen for the milkman ?'

'But isn't Mrs. Cockles here ?' asked Pip. She always

comes on Tuesdays, doesn't she ?'

'She does, usually,' said Mrs. Moon. 'But she hasn't turned up yet, so I'm all on me own. I won't be above ten minutes gone—but I must get my kidneys.'

She disappeared. The children giggled. 'I hope the butcher hands her her kidneys all right,' said Larry. 'I shouldn't like to be without mine !'

'Idiot !' said Daisy. 'Come on now—we can really let ourselves go, now the house is empty !'

In the middle of all the hullabaloo, Pip heard a noise. He sat up, trying to push Fatty off him. 'Listen—is that the telephone ?' he asked.

It was. Goodness knows how long the bell had been ringing ! 'I'll go, if you like,' said Fatty, who knew that Pip hated answering the telephone. 'It's probably from the butcher to say he's sending Mrs. Moon's kidneys !'

He ran downstairs. He lifted the telephone receiver and spoke into it. 'Hallo !'

' 'Allo !' said a voice. 'Can I speak to Mrs. Hilton, please ?'

'She's out,' said Fatty.

'Oh, Well, is Mrs. Moon there ?' said the voice. 'It's Mrs. Cockles speaking.'

'Oh, Mrs. Cockles, this is Frederick Trotteville here, answering the phone for Philip Hilton,' said Fatty. 'Mrs. Moon has just gone down to—er—fetch her kidneys. Can I give her a message when she comes back ?'

'Oh yes, Master Frederick, please,' said Mrs. Cockles. 'Tell her, I'm that sorry I can't come to-day— but my sister's upset and I've had to go round to her. Tell Mrs. Moon she's had one of them there letters. She'll know what I mean.'

Fatty at once pricked up his ears. 'One of them there letters !' That could only mean one thing surely—that the wicked letter-writer had been busy again as usual, and had sent a letter to somebody else—Mrs. Cockles's sister this time. His brain worked quickly.

'Mrs. Cockles, I'm so sorry to hear that,' he said in a rather pompous, grown-up tone. 'Very sorry indeed. So upsetting, those anonymous letters, aren't they ?'

'Oh—you've heard about them then,' said Mrs. Cockles. 'Yes, right down wicked they are. Upset folks properly they do. And to think as my pore innocent sister should have had one of them. Mrs. Moon will be sorry to hear that—not that she ever had much time for my pore sister, they never did get on, but Mrs. Moon she knows how it upsets people to get one of these here nonminus letters, and she'll understand why I've got to be with my pore sister this day instead of coming to help as I usually do. . . .'

This was all said without Mrs. Cockles taking a single breath, and Fatty felt slightly dazed. He felt that if he didn't interrupt, Mrs. Cockles might quite well go on for another ten minutes.

'Mrs. Cockles, do you think you sister would let me see the letter ?' he asked. 'I'm—er—very interested in these things—and, as you perhaps know, I am quite good at solving mysteries, and . . .'

'Yes, I've heard how you found Lady Candling's cat for her, and found the real guilty person too, said Mrs. Cockles. 'You come round to my sister's if you like, and she'll show you the letter. She lives at 9, Willow Lane. I'll be there. And give my regrets to Mrs. Moon and say I'll be along on Thursday for sure.'

Fatty replaced the receiver and rushed upstairs in the greatest excitement. He burst into the play-room and stood dramatically in the doorway.

'What do you *think* !' he said. 'There's been another of those beastly letters—sent to Mrs. Cockles's sister ! She got it this morning and is all upset and that's why Mrs. Cockles didn't turn up to help Mrs. Moon ! And Mrs. Cockles said if I go round to her sister's, she'll show me the letter. I simply *must* find out where it was posted and when.'

'Golly !' said every one.

'Let me come too,' said Pip.

'No. Best for only one of us to go,' said Fatty. 'Give Mrs. Moon this message when she comes back, Pip— say that Mrs. Cockles rang up and said she had to go to her sister, who was upset because she'd had a nasty letter. Don't let on that you know any more than that.'

'Right,' said Pip. 'Well, you hop off now, Fatty, before old Goon gets going on the job. He'll be round at Mrs. Cockle's sister in no time, as soon as he hears about the letter.'

Fatty shot off. He knew where Willow Lane was. He found number 9 and went to the little front door. It was a dirty, untidy little plac. He rapped on the wooden door.

'Come in !' called Mrs. Cockles's voice. 'Oh, it's you, Master Frederick. Well, my sister says she won't show you the letter. She says what's in it isn't for any one to read but me and the police. And I won't say but what she's right, now I've read the letter properly.'

Fatty was most bitterly disappointed. 'Oh, I say !' he said. 'You might just let me have a squint. I've seen all the others. Go on, be a sport and let me see it.'

Mrs. Cockles's sister was a fat, undity woman, who breathed very loudly through her mouth and talked through her nose.

''Taint fit for a child to read,' she said. 'It's a right down spiteful letter, and not a word of truth in it, neither!'

'I'm not a child !' said Fatty, making himself as tall as he could. You can trust me to read the letter and not say a word to anyone. I'm—er—I'm investigating the case, you see.'

Mrs. Cockles was very much impressed. But she still agreed with her sister that the letter was not one for him to read. Fatty, of course, was not in the least curious about its content—but he did badly want to see the printing and, of course, the envelope.

'Well—could I just see the envelope ? he asked. 'That would do quite well.'

Neither Mrs. Cockles nor Mrs. Lamb, her sister, could see any reason why he should not see the envelope. They handed it to him. Fatty looked at it eagerly to make out the post-mark.

But there was none ! There was no stamp, no post-mark ! Fatty stared in surprise.

'But—it didn't come by post !' he said.

'I never said it did,' said Mrs. Lamb. 'It come this morning, very early—about half-past six, I reckon. I heard something being pushed under the door, but I was too sleepy to get up. So I didn't get it till about half-past eight—and then I was that upset, I sent for Mrs. Cockles here. And you come at once, didn't you, Kate ?'

'Course I did,' said Mrs. Cockles. 'Only stopped to have a word with Mr. Goon about it. He'll be along soon to have a look at the letter too.'

Fatty felt slightly alarmed. He didn't want to bump into Clear-Orf at the moment. He stared hard at the envelope once more. The name and address were printed in capital letters again, and the square envelope was the same as the others that had been used. Fatty took his note-book out of his pocket and looked at the page headed CLUES.

He compared the tracing of the word PETERS-WOOD with the same word on the envelope. Yes there was no doubt at all, but that the same hand wrote both words. They were exactly alike.

Fatty handed the envelope back to Mrs. Lamb. He had got from it all he wanted. He didn't want to see the letter inside. He could imagine it—a few sentences of spite and hurtfulness, with perhaps a little truth in them. He had enough to puzzle himself with—here was the usual letter, received on a Tuesday morning—but this time not through the post, and not from Sheepsale. Funny !

'Well, I'll be going,' said Fatty. 'Thanks for showing me the envelope, Mrs. Lamb I'm so sorry you had one of these beastly letters. I shan't rest till I find out who is the writer of them.'

'Mr. Goon, he's on to them to,' said Mrs. Cockles. 'Says he's got a very good idea who it is, too.'

Fatty doubted that. He was sure that Mr. Goon was as puzzled as he was. He said good-bye and went out of the dirty little room.

But coming in at the front gate was the burly figure of Mr. Goon ! Fatty was annoyed. He tried to get out of the gate before Mr. Goon came in, but the policeman, surprised and exasperated at seeing Fatty there, caught hold of his arm. He pulled the boy inside the cottage.

'Has this boy been interfering with the Workings of the Law ?' he demanded, in an angry voce. 'What's he doing here, that's what I want to know ?'

Mrs. Lamb was afraid of Mrs. Goon, but Mrs. Cockles was not.

'He's not been interfering,' she said. 'Only taking a friendly interest like.'

'How did he know that Mrs. Lamb had received one of these here letters ?' inquired Mrs. Goon, still in a furious voice.

'Well, I had to ring up Mrs. Moon to tell her as how I wouldn't be along this morning, because my sister had had a letter,' said Mrs. Cockles. 'And Master Frederick, he happened to be there, and he took the message. And he said he knew all about the letters and would like to see this one, and I knew he wasn't half-bad at snooping out things, so . . .'

'Mrs. Lamb, you didn't show this interfering boy that letter before you showed it to me, did you ?' thundered Mr. Goon.

'Well—well, sir—he did say as he's seen them all,' stammered poor Mrs. Lamb, frightened out of her life. 'So I thought there wouldn't be much harm. I only showed him the envelope though, Mr. Goon, sir.'

Mr. Goon turned his frog-like gaze on to Fatty. 'What's that mean—that you've seen *all* the letters ?' he demanded.

Mr. Goon caught hold of Fatty's arm

'They've been in my possesssion—never out of it for a minute. What you mean—you've seen them *all* ?'

'I must have been dreaming,' answered Fatty, in an amiable voice. This was the voice that drove poor Mr. Goon to fury. He snorted.

'You're telling untruths,' he said. 'Yes, you know you are. Them letters haven't been out of my possession, not for one minute !'

'Haven't they really ?' said Fatty. 'Well, I couldn't have seen them then.'

'Unless you know more about them than you make out !' said Mr. Goon, darkly and mysteriously, suddenly remembering how he had seen Fatty post a letter at Sheepsale the morning before. 'Ho, you're a deep one, you are—never know what your game is, I don't ! I wouldn't put anything past you, Master Frederick Trotteville !'

'Thank you, Mr. Theophilus Goon,' said Fatty, and grinned. Mr. Goon longed to box his ears. Then he suddenly remembered that those letters *had* been out of his possession once—that time when he had apparently dropped them in the road, after colliding with the red-haired telegraph-boy. He stared suspiciously at Fatty.

'That telegraph-boy your friend?' he asked suddenly. Fatty looked mildly surprised.

'What telegraph-boy ?' he asked.

'That red-haired fellow with the freckles,' said Mr. Goon.

'I'm afraid I've no red-haired, freckled telegraph-boy for a friend, much as I would like one,' said Fatty. 'But why all these questions about a telegraph-boy ?'

Mr. Goon wasn't going to tell him. But he made a mental

note to get hold of that telegraph-boy and ask him a few questions. Perhaps he and Fatty were in league together !

'Well, I'll go now,' said Fatty politely, 'unless you've got any more questions to ask me about telegraph-boys, Mr. Goon ? Oh—and would you like another clue ? Wait a bit, I'll see if I've got one about me !'

To Mr. Goon's rage he felt in his pockets and produced a doll's straw hat. 'Now was that a clue ?' murmured Fatty, but, seeing Mr. Goon gradually turning a familiar purple, he moved swiftly through the door.

'If you don't clear-orf,' said Mr. Goon, between his teeth, 'if you don't clear-orf . . .I'll . . .I'll . . .'

But Fatty had cleared-orf. He sprinted back to Pip's. The mystery of the letters was warming up again!

14   THREE MORE SUSPECTS

HE was soon back in the playroom, relating everything to the other. How they roared when they heard about Mr. Goon coming in and hearing that Fatty had seen all the letters!

'That must have given him a shock !' said Pip. 'He'll wonder for hours how you've seen them. I bet he'll go about looking for that telegraph-boy now—he knows he's the one who handed him the letters he was supposed to have dropped.'

'Well, he'll be lucky if he finds the telegraph-boy, even if he goes up to the post-office to look for him !' said Fatty. 'But I say—*now* we know why none of the bus passengers posted the letter! It was delivered by hand instead ! No wonder we didn't see any one popping the letter into Sheepsale post-box !'

'It must be some one who didn't catch the bus yesterday for some reason,' said Daisy thoughtfuly. 'We really must find out if any one who regularly catches that bus, didn't take it yesterday. If we can find out the person who didn't go as usual, we *may* have discovered who the letter-writer *is* !'

'Yes—you're right, Daisy,' said Larry. 'Shall one of us catch the 10.15 bus to-morrow, Fatty and ask the conductor a few questions ?'

'Perhaps we'd better not,' said Fatty. 'He might think it a bit funny, or think us cheeky, or something. I've got a better idea than that.'

'What ?' asked the others.

'Well, what about going in to see Miss Tremble this morning ?' said Fatty. 'We know she usually takes the Monday morning bus. We could get from her the names of all the people who always catch it at Peterswood. After all, it starts off by the church, and that's where she gets in. She must know everyone who takes it on Mondays.'

'Yes. Lets go and see her now,' aid Bets. 'Mrs. Moon is back with her kidneys, Fatty. She wasn't long. Pip gave her the message, and she said, 'Well, well, she wasn't surprised to hear that Mrs. Lamb had got one of those letters, she was the dirtiest, laziest woman in the village !'

'Well, I must say her cottage was jolly smelly,' said Fatty. 'Come on—let's go in next door. We'll ask Miss Trimble if she's seen your cat, Pip.'

'But Whiskers is here,' said Pip in surprise, pointing to the big black cat.

'Yes, idiot. But Miss Trimble's not to know that,' said Fatty. 'We've got to have *some* excuse for going in. She'll probably be picking flowers in the garden, or taking the dog for an airing. Let's look over the wall first.'

Their luck was in. Miss Trimble was in the garden, talking to Miss Harmer who looked after Lady Candling's valuable Siamese cats for her.

'Come on. We'll go up the front drive and round to where she's talking,' said Fatty. 'I'll lead the conversation round to the bus.'

They set off, and soon found Miss Trimble. Miss Harmer was pleased to see them too. She showed them all the blue-eyed cats.

'And you really must come and see the daffodils in the orchard,' said Miss Trimble, setting her glasses firmly on her nose. Bets gazed at them, hoping they would fall off.

They all trooped after her. Fatty walked politely beside her, holding back any tree-branches that might catch at her hair. She thought what a very well-mannered boy he was.

'I hope you found your mother well on Monday,' said Fatty.

'Not so very well,' said Miss Trimble. 'She's got a bad heart, you know, poor old lady. She's always so glad to see me on Mondays.'

'And you must quite enjoy Mondays too,' said Fatty. 'Such a nice trip up to Sheepsale, isn't it, and such a fine little market !'

Miss Trimble's glasses fell off, and dangled on the end of their little gold chain. She put them on again, and smiled at Fatty.

'Oh yes, I always enjoy my Mondays,' she said.

'I expect you know all the people who go in the bus!' said Daisy, feeling that it was her turn to say something now.

'Well, I do, unless there are strangers, and we don't get many of those,' said Miss Trimble. 'Mrs. Jolly always goes, of course—such a nice person. And that artist-girl goes too—I don't know her name—but she's always so sweet and polite.'

'Yes, we liked her too,' said Fatty. 'Did you see the man I sat by, Miss Trimble ? Such a surly fellow.'

'Yes. I've never seen him before,' said Miss Trimble. 'The vicar often gets on the bus at Buckle, and I usually have such a nice talk with him. Mr. Goon sometimes goes up on that bus too, to have a word with the policeman in charge of Sheepsale. But I'm always glad when he's not there, somehow.'

'I suppose one or two of the regular Monday bus-people weren't there yesterday, were they?' said Fatty innocently. 'I thought the bus would be much more crowded than it was.'

'Well, let me see now—yes, there *are* usually more people,' said Miss Trimble, her glasses falling off again. The children held their breath. Now they would perhaps hear the name of the wicked letter-writer !

'Anyone *we* know ?' asked Fatty.

'Well, I don't know if you know Miss Tittle, do you?' said Miss Trimble. 'She *always* goes up on a Monday, but she didn't yesterday. She's a dressmaker, you know, and goes up to Sheepsale House to sew all day Mondays.'

'Really ?' said Fatty. 'Is she a special friend of yours, Miss Trimble ?'

'Well, no,' said Miss Trimble. 'I can't say she is. She's like a lot of dressmarkers, you know—full of gossip and scandal—a bit spiteful, and I don't like that. It's not Christian, I say. She pulls people to pieces too much for my liking. Knows a bit too much about everybody !

The children immediately felt absolutely certain that Miss Tittle was the writer of those spiteful letters. She sounded exactly like them !

'Aren't the daffodils simply lovely ?' said Miss Trimble, as they came to the orchard.

'Glorious !' said Daisy. 'Let's sit down and enjoy them.'

They all sat down. Miss Trimble looked anxiously at the children and went rather red.

'I don't think I should have said that about Miss Tittle,' she said. 'I wasn't thinking. She sometimes comes here to sew for Lady Candling, you know, and I do find it very difficult not to be drawn into gossip with her—she asks me such questions ! She's coming here this week, I believe, to make up the new summer curtains—and I'm not looking forward to it. I can't bear all this nasty spitefulness.'

'No, I should think not,' said Bets, taking her turn at making a remark. 'You're not a bit like that.'

Miss Trimble was so pleased with this remark of Bets that she smiled, wrinkled her nose, and her glassses fell off.

'That's three times,' said Bets. Miss Trimble put back

her glasses and did not look quite so pleased. She couldn't bear Bets to count like that.

'We'd better be going,' said Fatty. Then a thought struck him. 'I suppose there aren't any other Monday regulars on that bus, Miss Tremble—Trimble, I mean ?'

'You seem very interested in that bus !' said Miss Trimble. 'Well, let me think. There's always old Nosey, of course. I don't know why he didn't go yesterday. He always goes up to the market.'

'Old Nosey ? Whoever is he ?' asked Fatty.

'Oh, he's the old fellow who lives with his wife in the caravan at the end of Rectory Field,' said Miss Trimble. 'Maybe you've never seen him.'

'Oh yes, I have ! Now I remember !' said Fatty. 'He's a little stooping fellow, with a hooked nose and a droopy little moustache, who goes about muttering to himself.

'He's called Nosey because he's so curious about everyone,' said Miss Trimble. 'The things he wants to know! How old my mother is—and how old I am too—and what Lady Candling does with her old clothes—and how much the gardener gets in wages. I don't wonder people call him Old Nosey.'

Fatty looked round at the others. It sounded as if old Nosey, too, might be the letter-writer. He might be a bit daft and write the letters in a sort of spiteful fun. Fatty remembered a boy at his school who had loved to find out the weak spots in the others, and tease them about them. It was quite likely that Old Nosey was the letter-writer !

'And then, of course, there's always Mrs. Moon, your cook, Pip,' said Miss Trimble, rather surprisingly. 'She always had Mondays off to go and see to her old mother, just like me—and I usually see her every single Monday. But I didn't see her yesterday.'

'Well, you see, our housemaid, Gladys, has gone away for a few days,' explained Pip. 'And so I suppose Mother couldn't let Mrs. Moon off for the day. Yes–now I think of it—Mrs. Moon does go off on Mondays.'

'Any one else a regular passenger on the bus ?' asked Larry.

'No, nobody,' said Miss Trimble. 'You *do* seem interested in that bus. But I'm sure you didn't come in here to ask me about that Monday morning bus, now did you ! What did you come to ask ?'

The children had forgotten what reason they were going to give ! Bets remembered just in time.

'Oh—we were going to ask if you'd seen our cat !' she said.

'So that's what you came in for !' said Miss Trimble. 'No—I'm afraid I haven't seen your cat. It's that big black one, isn't it ? I shouldn't think you need to worry about *him* ! He can look after himself all right.'

'I've no doubt he's indoors sitting by the fire this very minute,' said Pip, quite truthfully. 'Well, we must go, Miss Tremble.'

'Trimble, dear boy, not Tremble,' said Miss Trimble, her glasses falling off again. 'I simply cannot imagine why you keep making that mistake. Any one would think I was like an aspen leaf, all of a tremble !'

The children laughed politely at this small joke, said good-bye and went. They said nothing at all till they were safely in Pip's playroom with the door shut. Then they looked at one another in excitement.

'Well ! Three more really fine Suspects !' said Fatty, opening his notebook. 'Would you believe it ? I think there's no doubt that one of them is the letter-writer.'

'Not Mrs. Moon,' said Bets. 'She was so kind to Gladys. Gladys said so. She couldn't be mean to her and kind to her as well.'

'I suppose not,' said Fatty. 'But all the same she's going down on our list. Now then—Miss TittleTattle.'

The others laughed. 'Miss Tittle, not Tittle-Tattle !' said Pip.

'I know, idiot,' said Fatty. 'But I think Tittle-Tattle suits her jolly well. Miss Tittle—old Nosey—and Mrs. Moon. We're getting on. Now we'll have plenty more inquiries to make.'

'What inquiries ?' asked Pip.

'Well—we must try and find out if Old Nosey, Miss Tittle, and Mrs. Moon were out early this morning,' said Fatty. 'That letter was pushed under Mrs. Lamb's door at about half-past six. It was only just getting light then. If we can find out that any of those three were out early, we've got the right one !'

'However are you going to find *that* out ?' said Larry. 'I shouldn't have thought even you were clever enough for that, Fatty !'

'Well, I am !' said Fatty. 'And what's more I'll go and do it now—and come back and tell you all about it in an hour's time !'

15   FATTY MAKES A FEW ENQUIRIES

FATTY went off, whistling. The others watched him from the window. 'I suppose he's going to interview Old Nosey, Miss Tittle, and Mrs. Moon !' said Pip. 'He's a wonder ! Never turns a hair, no matter what he's got to do.'

'All the same, he won't find Mrs. Moon an easy one to interview,' said Larry. 'She doesn't seem to me to be in a very good temper to-day—because Mrs. Cockles hasn't turned up, I suppose.'

An hour went by. It was a quarter to one. The children went to the window and watched for Fatty. He came cycling up the drive—but dear me, how different he looked ! He had put on his red wig again, but with black eyebrows this time, and had reddened his face till it looked weather-beaten. He wore a dirty old suit and a butcher-boy apron round his waist !

But the children knew it was Fatty all right, by his whistle ! He stopped under their window. 'Any one about ?' he said. 'Shall I come up ?'

'It's safe,' said Pip, leaning out of the window. 'Mrs. Moon's in the back-yard.'

Fatty came up, looking a real, proper butcher-boy. It was amazing how he could alter even his expression when he was supposed to be somebody else. He took off his apron and wig, and looked a bit better.

'Well—what have you found out ?' said Larry eagerly. 'And why ever are you dressed like that ?'

'I've found out a lot,' said Fatty. 'But I don't know that I'm any further forward really ! I'll tell you everything. I'm dressed like this because it's natural for a butcher-boy to hang about and gossip.'

He opened his notebook, and turned to the pages headed 'SUSPECTS.'

'Old Nosey,' he began. 'Old Nosey was up and about before half-past six this morning, with his dog, Lurcher. He left his caravan and went down Willow Lane, and into the village. He was back at eight o'clock.'

He turned over another page.

'Miss Tittle,' he said. 'Miss Tittle was about with her dog at half-past six, as she is every single morning. She lives in a turning off Willow Street. She always wears an old red shawl in the mornings.'

'Mrs. Moon,' went on Fatty, turning over a page again. 'Mrs. Moon was out this morning, early and was seen talking to Old Nosey. Well, there you are, Find-Outers. What do you make of that? Every one of our three Suspects could have popped that letter under the door!'

'But, Fatty—however did you find out all this?' said Bets, in great admiration. 'You really are a most marvellous Find-Outer.'

'Elementary, my dear Bets!' said Fatty, putting his notebook down. 'You know the field opposite Willow Lane? Well, old Dick the shepherd lives there in a little hut. I noticed him this morning. So all I had to do was to go and engage him in conversation, and ask him a few innocent questions—and out it all came! Old Dick was wide awake at five o'clock—always is—and he takes a great interest in the people that pass up and down by his field. They're about all he has to see, except his sheep. He says Nosey's always up and about at unearthly hours— a poacher most likely. He's a gypsy anyway. And apparently Miss Tittle always takes her dog for a trot early in the morning. So there's nothing unusual about that. He says he saw Mrs. Moon quite distinctly, and heard her voice too, talking to Old Nosey.'

'I'm sure it's Mrs. Moon!' said Larry. 'She *never* goes out so early, surely. I've heard your mother say she gets up too late, Pip.'

'Sh! Here she comes, to say our lunch is ready,' said Pip warningly. Sure enough, it was Mrs. Moon.

She put her head in at the door. 'Will you come now, Master Philip?' she said, 'I've put your lunch and Miss Bets in the dining-room.'

'Thank you, Mrs. Moon,' said Pip. Then, on a sudden impulse, he called out.

'I say, Mrs. Moon—isn't it queer, the old shepherd told Fatty that he saw you out at halfpast six this morning! He must be dreaming, mustn't he!'

There was a sudden pause. Mrs. Moon looked startled and surprised.

'Well there now,' she said at last. 'Who would have thought any one'd be peeping out at that time of day. Yes, it's quite right. I *was* out early this morning. You see, I usually go up to see my old mother at Sheepsale on a Monday, and I couldn't let her know in time that I wasn't coming yesterday. I knew she'd be worrying, and I remembered that Old Nosey, the gypsy fellow, might be going up to-day, so I got out early and gave him a note for my mother, and a packet of food in case she hasn't been able to get some one to buy any for her. He'd be taking the 10.15 bus.'

'Oh,' said the children, really quite relieved at this explanation.

'So that's it !' said Pip, without thinking.

'That's what ?' asked Mrs. Moon sharply.

'Nothing,' said Pip hastily, feeling a nudge from Fatty. 'Nothing at all !'

Mrs. Moon looked at the children curiously. Fatty got up. He didn't want to make Mrs. Moon suspicious about anything.

'Time I went,' he said. 'Your lunch will get cold, Pip and Bets if you don't go and have it. See you later.'

'Here's your notebook, Fatty !' Bets called after him, as he went downstairs. 'Your precious notebook with all its Clues and Suspects ! Fatty, are you going to write up the case again ? You've got some more to put down now, haven't you ?'

'Chuck the book down to me,' said Fatty. 'Yes, I'll write up the case as far as it's gone. I bet old Goon would like to see my notes !'

He went out of the garden-door with Larry and Daisy. Fatty did not put on his wig or apron agin. He stuffed them into his bicycle basket. 'Good thing I'd taken them off before Mrs. Moon came in,' he said. 'She'd have wondered why you were hobnobbing with the butcher-boy !'

'Fatty, who do you think is the letter-writer ?' said Daisy, who was burning with curiosity. 'I think it's Mrs. Moon. I do really.'

'I do too,' said Larry. 'But I don't see how we are to get any proof.'

'Yes, it certainly *might* be Mrs. Moon,' said Fatty thoughtfully. 'You remember that Pip told us she wanted her niece to come here ? She might have got Gladys out of the way for that. And yet—there are all the other letters too. Whoever wrote them must be a bit mad, I think.'

'What do we do next ?' asked Larry.

'I think we'll try and find out a bit more about Mrs. Moon,' said Fatty. 'We'll meet at Pip's at half-past two.'

When they arrived back at Pip's, they found him and Bets in a great state of excitment.

'What do you think ! Old Clear-Orf is here and he's been going for Mrs. Moon like anything !' cried Pip. 'We heard a lot of it, because the kitchen window's open and it's just under our playroom !'

'What's he been going at her for ?' asked Fatty.

'Well, apparently she used to live near the Home where Gladys was,' said Pip. 'And once she was working there as cook, and she got the sack because the girls complained of her bad temper. Maybe Gladys was one of those that complained ! Old Clear-Orf has been making inquiries himself, I suppose, and when he found out that Mrs. Moon actually knew the Home Gladys had been in, I suppose he came over all suspicious. He shouted at her like anything—and she shouted back !'

A noise of voices arose again. The children leaned out of the window.

'And what right have you got to come here and talk to an innocent woman like you have !' shouted Mrs. Moon. 'I'll have the law on you !'

'I *am* the Law,' came Mr. Goon's ponderous voice.

'I'm not accusing you of anything, Mrs. Moon, please understand that. I'm just asking you a few questions in the ordinary way of business, that's all. Routine questions is what we call them. Checking up on people, and finding out about them. Clearing them if they're innocent—as I've no doubt you are. You didn't ought to go on like this just because the Law asks you a few civil questions !'

'There's others you could well ask questions of,' said Mrs. Moon darkly. 'Yes, others I could tell you of.'

I've got a list of people I'm asking questions of,' said Mr. Goon. 'And all I hope is they'll be more civil than you've been. You don't make a good impression, Mrs. Moon, you don't, and that's flat.'

Whereupon Mr. Goon took his departure, and cycled slowly and heavily up the drive, the back of his neck looking bright red with rage.

'Old Goon's a bit brighter than we think,' said Fatty. 'He seems to have got his list of Suspects just as we have—and Mrs. Moon is down on his too !'

'I thought when he saw you posting that letter yesterday at Sheepsale he'd suspect *you* !' said Larry.

'Oh, I think he's sure I'm "messing about" somehow, as he puts it,' said Fatty. 'He's probably expecting some one to get a stupid letter from *me*, as well as from the real letter-writer. Well—I've a jolly good mind to let him have one !'

'Oh no, Fatty !' said Daisy.

Fatty grinned. 'No, I didn't mean it. Well, let's go out into the garden, shall we ? We'll go up to that old summer-house. I'll write up my notes there, whilst you all read or do something. It's too hot to stay indoors.'

They all went up to the summer-house. It backed on to the next-door garden, and was a nice, secluded little place, well away from the house. The children pulled some early radishes from the garden and washed them, meaning to nibble them all the afternnon.

They all talked hard about their mystery. They discussed everything and everybody. They read out loud what Fatty had written. It sounded very good indeed. He had even written up the interview between Mr. Goon and Mrs. Moon that afternoon. It began :

> 'Said Mr. Goon
> To Mrs. Moon'

and went on in such a funny strain that the children roared.

Then, quite suddenly, they heard voices very near them. They stopped their talk, startled. Who could be so near ?

They peeped out of the summer-house. They saw Mrs. Moon, with some lettuces in her hand, talking to a stranger over the wall, almost within touch of their summer-house.

'Well, that's what I always say, Miss Tittle,' they heard Mrs. Moon say. 'If a thing's too tight, it's not worth wearing!'

'You're quite right,' said the little, neat woman looking over the wall. 'But people will have their things made so tight. Well, do come in and see me about that dress of yours, Mrs. Moon, sometime. I'd enjoy a good talk with you.'

'I bet she would,' whispered Daisy. 'The two of them together would just about pull every one in Peterswood to pieces !'

'Miss Tittle didn't look a very nice person,' said Bets, watching Mrs. Moon go down the path with her lettuces.

She had obviously just been up the kitchen garden nearby to pull them.

'I suppose you realize that we've been talking very loudly, and that both Miss Tittle and Mrs. Moon could have heard every word, if they'd been listening ?' said Fatty, with a groan. 'I never thought of any one coming up here. Miss Tittle must have been just the other side of the wall, and Mrs. Moon must have come up to get the lettuces. They grow quite near the summer-house. Now both will be on their guard, if they've heard what we've been saying !'

'They won't have heard !' said Pip.

'They may quite well have done,' said Fatty. 'What idiots we are. Really ! Giving all our clues and facts away at the tops of our voices. And Bets reading out loud from my notes !'

'Why didn't Buster bark ?' said Bets.

'Well, he knows Mrs. Moon all right and wouldn't bark if she came by,' said Fatty. 'And I don't expect he bothers about any one in the next garden. Do you, Buster, old fellow ?'

'Woof,' said Buster lazily. He was lying in a patch of sun and it was pleasantly warm on him. He cocked his ears up, hoping to hear the magic word 'Walk.'

He soon heard it. 'I vote we go for a walk,' said Larry. 'It's getting stuffy here. let's go down to the river and watch the swans. We'll take some bread.'

Pip asked Mrs. Moon for some bread. She seemed sulky and upset. 'No wonder,' thought Pip, 'after having Mr. Goon bellowing at her !'

They had a lovely time by the river. they sauntered

back to tea, but parted at Pip's, because each had to get back home for tea that afternoon.

'See you to-morrow,' said Fatty. 'We seem to be rather stuck again, don't we ? This mystery wants oiling a bit ! Well—maybe something will happen to-morrow!'

Fatty was quite right. Plenty happened—and it was very exciting too !

16   MR. GOON IS PUZZLED

FATTY thought he would wear his butcher-boy disguise the next morning, in case he had to go and do a bit more snooping or interviewing. It was a simple disguise, and very effective. He put on his red wig, with no cap. He adjusted the black eyebrows and made his face red. Then, with his striped apron tied round his middle, he set off to Pip's.

Mrs. Hilton saw him as he flashed by the window. 'Ah, the butcher-boy,' she thought. 'Now Mrs. Moon won't have to go and fetch the meat again.'

The others greeted Fatty with delight. They were always thrilled when he disguised himself. He pulled off his wig, eyebrows, and apron when he got up into the playroom in case Mrs. Hilton should come in and see him.

He had no sooner done this than a great commotion began downstairs. The children listened, quite startled. They heard wails and groans, and somebody speaking sharply, then more wails.

They went to the head of the stairs and listened. It's Mrs. Moon—and Mother,' said Pip' 'What-ever is happening ? Mrs. Moon is crying and howling like anything and Mother is trying to make her stop. Gracious, what can be the matter ?'

'Perhaps Mother's discovered that Mrs. Moon is the bad letter-writer !' suggested Bets, looking rather scared.

'I'll go down and see what's up,' said Fatty, rising to the occasion as usual. He went down-stairs quietly. He heard Mrs. Hilton's stern voice.

'Now Mrs. Moon, you are not to go on like this. I won't have it ! Pull yourself together at once !'

'Oh Mam, to think I'd get one of those nasty letters!' wailed Mrs. Moon's voice. 'And such a spiteful one too ! Look here what it says.

'I don't want to see, Mrs. Moon. Pay no attention to it,' said Mrs. Hilton. 'You know quite well it is only something written out of somebody's spiteful imagination. Let Mr. Goon see it, and then forget all about it.'

'That Mr. Goon !' wailed Mrs. Moon. 'Didn't he come here yesterday and tell me I might be one of them he suspects could have written the letters-me, a law-abiding, peaceful woman that never did no one no harm. Ooooooo-o-oh !'

'Pull yourself together at once,' said Mrs. Hilton sharply !' You're getting hysterical and I won't have it! When did the letter come ?'

'Just this minute as ever was !' wailed Mrs. Moon. 'Somebody pushed it in at the kitchen door, and I picked it up and opened it—and there was that nasty spiteful

message—oh, to think somebody could write to me like
that, me that hasn't an enemy in the world.'

'Somebody pushed it in just *now* ?' said Mrs. Hilton
thoughtfully.'Well now—I saw the butcher-boy coming
by my window a minute ago'.

'He never came to my back door !' declared Mrs.
Moon. 'Never left any meat or nothing.'

'Strange,' said Mrs. Moon. 'Could it possibly have
been that boy who delivered the note—for somebody
else? Well, we can easily make inquiries at the
butcher's.'

Fatty wished heartily that he hadn't put on his
butcher-boy disguise. He must hide it well away when
he went upstairs.

'I'll go and telephone to Mr. Goon now,' said Mrs.
Hilton. 'Make yourself a cup of tea, Mrs. Moon, and try
and be sensible.'

Fatty shot upstairs as Mrs. Hilton came out into the
hall to telephone. The others clutched him.

'What's the row about ?' they asked. 'Quick, tell us!'.

'What do you think!' said Fatty. Mrs. Moon's had
one of those letters—delivered by hand a few minutes
ago. We might any of us have seen who it was that left
it here—but we didn't. But your mother spotted me in
my butcher-boy disguise, Pip, and that's a pity, because
she thinks *I'm* the one that delivered the letter !'

'Mrs. *Moon's* had a letter !' said Larry, and gave a low
whistle. '

Well, that rules her out then. That leaves only Nosey
and Miss Tittle'.

'Let's watch for Mr. Goon,' said Bets. So they

watched. He came cycling up the drive and dismounted by the front door. Mrs. Hilton let him in. The children stood at the top of the stairs, but Mrs. Hilton, worried and puzzled, did not even see them.

'I sent for you to say that Mrs. Moon has now had one of those unpleasant letters,' said Mrs. Hilton 'She is naturally very upset.'

'Well, Madam, I may tell you that I've had one too, this morning !' said Mr.Goon. 'It's getting beyond a joke, this is. I found mine in the letter-box this morning. Course, it may have been delivered in the dark of night, probably was. Making fun of the Law like that. Things have come to a pretty pass if the Law can be treated like that !'.

'It's very worrying,' said Mrs. Hilton. 'I can't imagine anyone wanting to send *you* that kind of letter, Mr. Goon.'

'Ah, no doubt the wrong-doer knows I'm on their track,' said Mr.Goon. 'Thinks to put me off, no doubt ! Tells me I'm a meddler and a muddler ! Ah, wait till I get me hands on them !'

'Well—come and see Mrs. Moon,' said Mrs. Hilton.'Please handle her carefully, Mr. Goon. She's almost hysterical.'

Obviously Mr. Goon couldn't handle a hysterical person, judging by the angry voices soon to be heard from the kitchen. The door opened again at last and Mr. Goon came out into the hall, looking extremely flustered, to find Mrs. Hilton, who had retired to the drawing-room.

'And that'll teach you to come pestering and accusing a poor, innocent woman !' Mrs. Moon's voice came from the kitchen. 'Pestering me yesterday like you do—and me struck all of a heap to-day!'.

Mr.Goon heard next about the red-headed butcher-boy, who had so mysteriously ridden up and left no meat, and had apparently departed without being seen.

Mr. Goon immediately thought of the red-headed telegraph-boy. 'Funny goings-on !' he said to himself. 'Them dropped letters now—and that telegraph-boy picking them up—and now this red-headed butcher-boy, without his meat—and maybe delivering that letter to Mrs. Moon. This wants looking into.'

'The five children are upstairs,' said Mrs. Hilton. 'I don't know if you want to ask them if they saw the butcher-boy. They may give you a few more details.'

'I'll see them,' said Mr. Goon, and went upstairs to the playroom. When he got there the children were apparently playing a game of snap. They looked up as Mr. Goon walked heavily into the room.

'Good morning,' he said. 'Did any of you see a red-headed butcher-boy coming along here this morning ?'

'Yes, I saw him,' said Pip with a grin.

'Ho, you did ! What did he do ? asked Mr. Goon.

'Just rode up the drive,' said Pip.

'And rode down again at once, I suppose,' said Mr.Goon.

'No. I didn't see him ride down,' said Pip. Nobody had apparently. Mr. Goon began to feel that this mysterious red-headed boy must be somewhere about the premises.

'He a friend of yours ? he said.

Pip hesitated. Fatty *was* his friend—and yet to say that

the butcher-boy was his friend would lead him into difficulties. Fatty saw him hesitate and came to the rescue.

'We've got no butcher-boy friends,' he said. 'And no telegraph-boy friends either. You remember you asked me that one too?'

'I'm not speaking to you,' said Mr. Goon, with a scowl. 'I'm speaking to Master Philip here. I'd like to get hold of them two red-headed lads! And I will too, if I have to go to the post-office and speak to the postmaster, and ask at every butcher's in the town!'

'There are only two butchers.' said Pip.

'Mr. Goon, I'm so sorry to hear you've had one of those horrid letters too,' said Fatty earnestly. 'I can't think now anyone could have the nerve—er, I mean—the heart to write to you like that'.

'Like what? said Mr. Goon sharply.'What do you know about any letters I've had? I suppose you'll tell me next you've seen the letter and know what's in it hey?'

'Well, I can more or less guess,' said Fatty modestly.

'You tell me what was in that letter then,' said Mr. Goon, growing angry.

'Oh I couldn't,' said Fatty. 'Not with all the others here.' He didn't know of course, what was in the letter at all, beyond that Goon was a meddler and a muddler, but it was amusing to make the policeman think he did.

'Well, it wouldn't surprise me at all if *you* didn't write that there letter to me!' said Mr.Goon.

'It might not be the letter-writter at all—it might just be you!'

'Oh, you *couldn't* think that of me!' said Fatty,

looking pained. Larry and Daisy, rather alarmed, looked at him. They remembered how he had said he would love to write a letter to Mr. Goon. Surely he *hadn't*?

Mr. Goon departed, determined to run the red-headed butcher-boy, and the equally red-headed telegraph-boy to earth. Larry turned to Fatty.

'I say! You didn't really write to him did you, Fatty?'

'Of course not, silly! As if I'd send an anonymous letter to any one, even for fun!' said Fatty. But my word, fancy somebody delivering a letter right into the lion's mouth! To Goon himself. I can't see Miss Tittle doing that—or even Old Nosey the gypsy.'

'And now Mrs. Moon's ruled out,' said Larry. 'Gracious—it seems more of a muddle than ever, really it does. Got any ideas as to what to do next, Fatty?'.

'One or two,' said Fatty. I think it would be rather helpful to get specimens of Miss Tittle's writing and old Nosey's. Just to compare them with my tracing. That might tell us something.'

'But how in the world can you do that? said Daisy. 'I wouldn't be able to get Old Nosey's writing if I thought for a month!'

'Easy!' said Fatty. 'You wait and see!'

THE next day both Mr. Goon and Fatty were very busy. Fatty was trying to get specimens of Nosey's writing and Miss Tittle's and Mr. Goon was trying to trace the two red-headed boys.

Fatty pondered whether to disguise himself or not, and then decided that he would put on the red wig, red eyebrows, and freckles, and a round messenger-boy's hat. It was essential that people should think he was a delivery boy of some sort, in order for him to get specimens of their writing—or so Fatty worked it out.

He set off on his bicycle to the Rectory Field, where Old Nosey, the gypsy, lived in a dirty caravan with his wife. In this basket he carried a parcel, in which he had packed two of his father's old pipes, and a tin of tobacco he had bought. Larry met him as he cycled furiously down the village street, keeping a sharp look-out for Goon.

'Fatty!' said Larry, and then clapped his hand over his mouth, hoping that no passer-by had heard.

'Fathead !' said Fatty, stopping by Larry. 'Don't yell my name out when I'm in disguise ! Yell out Bert, or Alf, or Sid—anything you like, but not Fatty'.

'Sorry ! I did it without thinking,' said Larry. 'I don't think any one heard. What are you going to do, Fatty— er, I mean Sid ?'

'I'm going to deliver a parcel to Old Nosey,' said Fatty. From an Unknown friend ! And he's got to sign a receipt for it. See ?'

'Golly, you're clever,' said Larry, filled with admiration. 'Of course—you can easily get him to sign his name—and address too, I suppose by delivering a parcel to him and asking for a receipt ! I'd never have thought of that. Never.'

'I've put a couple of old pipes and some tobacco in,' said Fatty, with a grin. 'Nice surprise for Old Nosey ! I'm delivering a parcel to Miss Tittle too—and one to Mrs. Moon later. I've a feeling that if we've got specimens of all three in the way of hand-writing, we shall soon be able to spot the real letter-writer ! I'm going to ask them to give me a receipt in capital letters, of course.'

'Good for you,' said Larry. 'I'll tell Pip and Bets to look out for you later—delivering something to Mrs. Moon!'

Fatty rode off, whistling. He soon came to Rectory Field. He saw the caravan standing at the end, its little tin chimney smoking. Mrs. Nosey was outside, cooking something over a fire, and Nosey was sitting beside it, sucking at an empty pipe. Fatty rode over the field-path and jumped off his bicycle when he came to Nosey.

'Good morning,' he said. 'Parcel for you ! Special delivery !'

He handed the parcel to the surprised Old Nosey. The gypsy took it and turned it round and round, trying to feel what was inside. 'Anythink to pay ? asked Mrs. Nosey.

'Good Morning. Parcel for you'

'No. But I must have a receipt, please,' said Fatty, briskly, and whipped out a notebook, in which was printed in capital letters :

RECEIVED, ONE PARCEL,

by . . . .

'Will you sign your name and address there, please, in capital letters ?' he asked, showing Nosey where he meant.

'I'm not signing nothing,' said Nosey, not looking at Fatty.

'Well, if you want the parcel, you'll have to sign for it,' said Fatty. Always get a receipt, you know. It's the only thing I've got, to show I've delivered the parcel. See ?'

'*I'll* sign it,'said Mrs. Nosey, and held out her hand for the pencil.

'No,' said Fatty. 'The parcel is for your husband. I'm afraid he must sign it, Madam.'

'You let me,' said Mrs. Nosey. 'Go on—you give it to me to sign. It don't matter which of us does it.'

Fatty was almost in despair. Also he thought it a very suspicious sign that Nosey didn't seem to want to sign his name and address in capital letters. It rather looked as if he was afraid of doing so.

'I shall have to take the parcel back if your husband doesn't give me a proper receipt fot it.' he said, in as stern a voice as he could manage. 'Got to be business-like over these things, you know. Pity—it smells like tobacco.'

'Yes, it do,' said Old Nosey, and sniffed the parcel eagerly. 'Go on, wife, you sign for it.'

'I tell you,' began Fatty. But Nosey's wife pulled at his elbow. She spoke to him in a hoarse whisper.

'Don't you go bothering 'im. 'E can't write nor read !'

'Oh,' said Fatty blankly, and let Mrs. Nosey sign a receipt without further objection. He could hardly read what she wrote, for she put half the letters backwards, and could not even spell Peterswood.

Fatty cycled off, thinking. So Old Nosey couldn't write. Well, he was ruled out too, then. That really only left Miss Tittle—because Mrs. Moon had had one of the letters and could be crossed off the List of Suspects.

He went home and fetched a cardboard box into which he had packed a piece of stuff he had bought from the draper's that morning. He was just in time to catch Miss Tittle setting out to go for the day to Lady Candling's again.

'Parcel for you,' said Fatty briskly. 'Special delivery. Will you please sign for it—here—in capital letters for clearness—name *and* address, please'.

Miss Tittle was rather surprised to receive a parcel by special delivery, when she was not expecting one, but she supposed it was something urgent sent to be altered by one of her customers. So she signed for it in extremely neat capital letters, small and beautiful like her stitches.

'There you are,' she said. 'You only just caught me ! Good morning.'

'That was easy !' thought Fatty, as he rode away. 'Now—I wonder if it's really necessary to get Mrs. Moon's writing ? Better, I suppose, as she's been one of the Suspects. Well, here goes!'

He rode up the drive of Pip's house. Pip and the

others were lying in wait for him, and they called out in low voices as he went past.

'Ho there, Sid !'

'Hallo, Bert !'

'Wotcher, Alf !'

Fatty grinned and went to the back door. He had a small and neat parcel this time, beautifully wrapped up and tied with string and sealed. It really looked a very exciting parcel.

Mrs. Moon came to the kitchen door, 'Parcel for you,' said Fatty, presenting it to her. 'Special delivery. Sign for it here, please, in capital letters for clearness, name and address'.

'Me hands are all over flour,' said Mrs. Moon. 'You just sign it for me, young man. Now who can that parcel be from, I wonder !'

''Fraid you'll have to sign it yourself,' said Fatty. Mrs. Moon made an exasperated noise and snatched the pencil from Fatty's hand. She went and sat down at the table and most laboriously pencilled her name and address. But she mixed up small letters and capital letters in a curious way. The receipt said :

RECEIVED, ONE PARCEL

by. . . . .

WInnIe MOOn,

ReDhoUSe

peTeRSWOOD

'Thank you,' said Fatty, looking at it closely. 'But you've mixed up small letters and capital ones, Mrs. Moon ! Why did you do that ?'

'I'm no writer !' said Mrs. Moon, annoyed. 'You take that receipt and be off. Schooling in my days wasn't what it is now, when even a five-year-old knows his letters.'

Fatty went off. If Mrs. Moon didn't very well know the difference between small and capital letters, he didn't see how she could have printed all those spiteful anonymous letters. Anyway, he didn't really suspect her. He thought about things as he rode down the drive and back through the village. Nosey couldn't write. Rule him out. Mrs. Moon couldn't have done it either. Rule her out. That only left Miss Tittle—and the difference between her small and beautiful printing and the untidy, laboured scrawl of the nasty letters was amazing.

'I can't think it can be *her* writing, in those letters,' thought Fatty. 'Well, really, this case is getting more and more puzzling. We keep getting very good ideas and clues-and then one by one they all fizzle out. Not one of our Suspects really seems possible now—though I suppose Miss Tittle is the likeliest.'

He was so deep in thought that he didn't look where he was going, and he almost ran over a dog. It yelped so loudly with fright that Fatty, much concerned, got off his bicycle to comfort it.

'What you doing to make that dog yelp like that ?' said a harsh voice suddenly, and Fatty looked up, started, to see Mr. Goon standing over him.

'Nothing, sir,' stammered Fatty, pretending to be scared of the policeman. A curious look came into Mr. Goon's eyes—so curious that Fatty began to feel *really* scared.

Mr. Goon was gazing at Fatty's red wig. He looked at Fatty's messenger-boy hat. He looked very hard indeed. Another red-headed boy ! Why, the village seemed full of them.

'You come-alonga me !' he said suddenly, and clutched hold of Fatty's arm. 'I want to ask you a few questions, see ? You just come-alonga me !'

'I've done nothing,' said Fatty, pretending to be a frightened messenger-boy. 'You let me go, sir. I ain't done nothing.'

'Then you don't need to be scared,' said Mr. Goon. He took firm hold of Fatty's arm and led him down the street to his own small house. He pushed him inside, and took him upstairs to a small box-room, littered with rubbish of all kinds.

'I've been looking for red-headed boys all morning !' said Mr. Goon grimly. 'And I haven't found the ones I want. But maybe *you*'ll do instead ! Now you just sit here, and wait for me to come up and question you. I'm tired of reheaded boys, I am—butting in and out— picking up letters and delivering letters and parcels— and disappearing into thin air. Ho yes, I'm getting a bit tired of these here red-headed boys !'

He went out, shut the door and locked it. He clumped downstairs, and Fatty heard him using the telephone though he couldn't hear what he said.

Fatty looked round quickly. It was no use trying to get out of the window, for it looked on to the High Street and heaps of people would see him trying to escape that way and give the alarm.

No—he must escape out of the locked door, as he had done once before when an enemy had locked him in. Ah, Fatty know how to get out of a locked room ! He felt in his pocket and found a folded newspaper there. It was really amazing what Fatty kept in his pocket ! He opened the newspaper, smoothed it out quite flat, and pushed it quietly under the crack at the bottom of the door.

Then he took a small roll of wire from his pocket, and straightened one end of it. He inserted the end carefully into the lock. On the other side, of course, was the key that Mr. Goon had turned to lock the door.

Fatty jiggled about with the piece of wire, pushing and moving the key a little. Suddenly, with a soft thud, it fell to the floor outside the door, on to the sheet of newspaper that Fatty had pushed underneath to the other side. He grinned.

He had left a corner of the newspaper on his side, and this he now pulled at very gently. The whole of the newspaper sheet came under the door bringing the key with it ! Such a clever trick and so simple, thought Fatty.

It took him just a moment to put the key into the lock his side, turn it and open the door. He took the key, stepped out softly, locked the door behind him and left the key in.

Then he stood at the top of the little stairway and listened. Mr. Goon was evidently in the middle of a long routine telephone call, which he made every morning about this time.

There was a small bathroom nearby. Fatty went into it and carefully washed all the freckles off his face. He removed his eyebrows and wig and stuffed them into his pocket. He took off his rather loud tie and put another one on, also out of his pocket.

Now he looked completely different. He grinned at himself in the glass. 'Disappearance of another red-headed boy,' he said, and crept downstairs as quietly as he could. Mr. Goon was still in his parlour, telephoning.

Fatty slipped into the small empty kitchen. Mrs. Cockles was not there to-day.

He went out of the back door, down the garden and into the lane at the end. He had to leave his bike behind —but never mind, he'd think of some way of getting it back! Off he went, whistling, thinking of the delight of the Find-Outers when he told them of his adventurous morning!

18   THE MYSTERY OF THE RED-HEADED BOYS

MR. GOON finished his telephoning and went clumping upstairs to give that boy What-For, and to Properly-Put-Him-Through-It. Mr. Goon was sick and tired of chasing after red-headed boys that nobody seemed to have heard of. Now that he had got one really under his thumb, he meant to keep him there and find out a great many things he was bursting to know.

He stood and listened outside the door. There wasn't a sound to be heard. That boy was properly scared. That's how boys should feel, Mr. Goon thought. He'd no time for boys—cheeky, don't care, whistling creatures! He cleared his throat and pulled himself up majestically to his full height. He was the Law, he was!

The key was in the lock. The door was locked all right. He turned the key and flung open the door. He trod heavily into the room, a pompous look on his red face.

There was nobody there. Mr. Goon stared all round the

room, breathing heavily. But there simply wasn't anybody there. There was nowhere to hide at all—no cupboard, no chest. The window was still shut and fastened. No boy had got out that way.

Mr. Goon couldn't believe his eyes. He swallowed hard. He'd been after two red-headed boys that morning, and nobody seemed to have heard of either of them—and now here was the third one gone. Disappeared. Vanished. Vamoosed. But WHERE? And HOW ?

Nobody could walk through a locked door. And the door *had* been locked, and the key his side too. But that boy had walked clean through that locked door. Mr. Goon began to feel he was dealing with some kind of Magic.

He walked round the room just to make sure that the boy hadn't squeezed into a tin or a box. But he had been such a plump boy ! Mr. Goon felt most bewildered. He wondered if he had got a touch of the sun. He had just reported over the telephone his capture of a red-headed boy, for questioning—and how was he to explain his complete disappearance ? He didn't feel that his superior officer would believe a boy could walk out of a locked door.

Poor Mr. Goon ! He had indeed had a trying morning- a real wild-goose chase, as he put it to himself.

He had first af all gone to the post-office to ask the post-master to let him talk to the red-headed telegraph-boy.

But when the telegraph-boy had come, he wasn't red-headed ! He was mousey-brown, and was a thin, under-sized little thing, plainly very frightened indeed to hear that Mr. Goon wanted to speak to him.

'This isn't the lad,' said Mr. Goon to the post master. 'Where's your other boy? The red-headed one ?'.

'We've only got the one boy,' said the post-master, puzzled. 'This is the one. We've never had a red-headed fellow, as far as I can remember. We've had James here for about fourteen months now'.

Mr. Goon was dumbfounded. No red-headed telegraph-boy ? Never had one ! Well then, where did that fellow come from ? Telegraph-boys were only attached to post-offices, surely.

'Sorry I can't help you,' said the post-master. 'But I do assure you we've got no red-headed boys at all here. But we've got a red-headed girl here – now would you like to see *her* ?'

'No,' said Mr.Goon,'This was a boy all right, and one of the civilest I ever spoke to—too civil by a long way. I see now ! Pah ! I'm fed up with this.

He went out of the post-office, feeling very angry, knowing that the post-master was thinking him slightly mad. He made his way to one of the butcher's, frowning. Just let him get hold of that there red-headed butcher-boy, delivering letters for the anonymous letter-writer. Ho, just let him ! He'd soon worm everything out of him !

Mr. Veale, the butcher, was surprised to see Mr. Goon. 'Bit of nice tender meat, sir, for you to-day ?' he asked, sharpening his knife.

'No thanks,' said Mr. Goon. 'I want to know if you've got a red-headed boy here, delivering your meat'.

'I've got no boy,' said Mr. Veale. 'Only old Sam, the fellow I've had for fifteen years. Thought you knew that'.

'Oh, I know old Sam,' said Mr. Goon. 'But I thought maybe you had a new boy as well. I expect it's the other butcher's delivery-boy I want.'

He went off to the other shop. This was a bigger establishment altogether. Mr. Cook, the owner, was there, cutting up meat with his two assistants.

'You got a boy here, delivering your meat for you?' asked Mr. Goon.

'Yes, two,' said Mr. Cook. 'Dear me. I hope they haven't either of them got into trouble, Mr. Goon. They're good boys, both of them.'

'One of them isn't,' said Mr. Goon grimly. 'Where are they? You let me see them.'

'They're out in the yard at the back packing their baskets with meat-deliveries,' said Mr. Cook. 'I'll come with you. Dear me. I do hope it's nothing serious.'

He took Mr. Goon out to the back. The policeman saw two boys. One was fair-haired with blue eyes and the other was black-haired dark as a gypsy.

'Well, there they are, Mr. Goon,' said Mr. Cook. 'Which of them is the rascal?'

The boys looked up, surprised. Mr. Goon took one look and scowled. 'They're neither of them the boy I want,' he said. 'I want a red-headed fellow.'

'There aren't any red-headed delivery-boys here, sir,' said the fair-haired lad. 'I know them all.'

Mr. Goon snorted and went back into the shop.

'Well, I'm glad it wasn't one of my boys,' said Mr. Cook. 'The fair-haired one is really a very clever fellow—he...'

But Mr. Goon didn't want to hear about any clever fair-haired boys. He wanted to see a red-headed one-and the more he tried to, the less likely it seemed he would ever find one.

He clumped out of the shop, disgusted. Who was the telegraph-boy ? Hadn't he seen him delivering a telegram to those children some time back—and again at night when he had bumped into him ? And what about that red-headed butcher-boy that Mrs. Hilton and Philip Hilton both said they had seen ? Who were these red-headed fellows flying around Peterswood, and not, apparently, living anywhere, or being known by any one?

Mr. Goon began to feel that he had red-headed boys on the brain, so, when he suddenly heard the loud yelping of a frightened dog, and looked up to see, actually to see a red-headed messenger-boy within reach of him, it was no wonder that he reached out and clutched that boy hard !

That was when Fatty had been trying to comfort the dog he had nearly run into. Mr. Goon had felt that it was a miracle to find a red-headed boy, even if he wasn't a telegraph-boy or a butcher-boy. He was red-headed, and that was enough!

And now he had lost that boy too. He had just walked out of a locked room and disappeared into thin air. Hey presto, he was there, and hey presto, he wasn't.

Mr.Goon forgot all about the boy's bicycle in his worry. It had been left out in the little front garden when he had pushed the boy into his house. The Policeman didn't even notice it there when he went out to get his mid-day paper.

Nor did he notice Larry waiting about at the corner.

But Larry had been posted there by Fatty to watch what Mr. Goon did with his bike. Fatty was afraid that Mr. Goon might make inquiries and find out who the right owner was, and he didn't want the policeman to know that.

Larry saw Mr. Goon come out. He imagined that having found that Fatty was gone, he would at least lock up his bicycle, and take a delight in doing it. He didn't realize poor Mr. Goon's stupefied state of mind. The puzzled man had sat down in his chair to think things out, but had got into such a muddle that he had decided to go out, get his paper and have a drink. Maybe he would feel better then.

Mr. Goon went out of his little front garden as if he was walking in a dream. He saw neither Larry nor the bicycle. He drifted on towards the paper-shop.

Larry gaped. Wasn't old Goon going to lock up the bicycle ? Surely he ought to do that ? Could he possibly have overlooked it ? It really did seem as if he had.

Mr. Goon went into the paper-shop. Larry acted like lightning ! He shot across the road, went into the little garden, took Fatty's bike out, mounted it and rode off at top speed. Nobody even saw him !

Mr. Goon got his paper, and had a little talk with the owner of the shop. As he went out again, he suddenly remembered the bicycle.

"Lawks ! I ought to have locked it up at once !' thought Mr.Goon, and began to hurry back to his house. 'How did I come to forget it ? I was that mazed.'

He hurried into his front garden—and then stopped short in dismay. The bicycle was gone ! It was now of course, half-way to Pip's house, ridden furiously by Larry, who was absolutely longing to know the whole of Fatty's story. But Mr. Goon didn't know that.

He gulped. This was getting too much for him. Three red-headed boys all vanishing into thin air—and now a completely solid bicycle doing the same thing. He supposed that red-headed fellow must have taken it somehow without his seeing-but how ?

'Gah !' said Mr. Goon, wiping his hot forehead. 'What with these here letters—and hysterical women— and red-headed disappearing fellows—and that cheeky toad, Frederick Trotteville—my life in Peterswood ain't worth living ! First one thing and then another. I'd like to talk to that Frederick Trotteville. I wouldn't put it past him to write me that cheeky anonymous letter. It's him that done that—I'd lay a million dollars it was. Gah !'

19   CLUES, REAL CLUES AT LAST !

THE Five-Find-Outers and Buster met in the little summer-house at the top of Pip's garden that afternoon. It was warm and sunny there, and they wanted to be quite alone and hear again and again of all that Fatty had done that morning—especially of his neat escape from Mr. Goon's boxroom.

'I simply can't *imagine* what he said when he unlocked the door and found you gone, Fatty' said Bets. 'I'd have loved to be there !'

Fatty showed them the two specimens of hand-writing he had taken from Miss Tittle and Mrs. Moon. He told them that Nosey couldn't write, so that ruled him out completely. 'And if you look at this receipt, which Mrs. Nosey signed, you'll see she could never have written those letters either, even if Nosey had told her what to put into them,' said Fatty.

'It's a funny thing,' said Daisy, 'we've had plenty of Suspects—but one by one we've had to rule them out. There honestly doesn't seem to be a single real Suspect left, Fatty.'

'And except for seeing the letters, we've got no real Clues either,' said Larry, 'I call this a most disappointing Mystery. The letter-writer went a bit mad this week, didn't he—or she—sending letters to Mrs. Lamb—and Mrs. Moon and Mr. Goon. Before that, as far as we know, only one a week was sent.'

'Isn't old Clear-Orf funny when I keep pretending I've got a new Clue ? said Fatty, grinning. 'Do you remember his face when I pulled old Waffles, the white rat, out of my pocket ? I just happened to have him there that day.'

Poor old Clear-Orf doesn't believe anything we say any more,' said Pip. 'I do wonder if he really suspects somebody of writing those letters—some one we don't know about ?'

'He may have some clues or ideas we haven't been able to get,' said Fatty. 'I shouldn't be surprised if he solves this Mystery after all—and not us'.

'Oh, *Fatty* !' cried every one in dismay.

'How *can* you say that ? said Bets. 'Wouldn't it be dreadful if he did—so that Inspector Jenks was pleased with him, and not with us.

Inspector Jenks was their very good friend, and had

always been very pleased with them because they had
managed to solve some curious mysteries in Peterswood
before. They had not seen him since the Christmas
holidays.

'Let's get out of this summer-house,' said Larry. 'It's
absolutely melting in here ! Fatty, don't forget to take
your red-haired wig and things back with you to-night.
This summer-house isn't an awfully safe hiding-place
for them. Pip's mother might easily walk in and see them
stuffed under the seat.'

'I'll remember,' said Fatty, yawning. 'Golly, it was
funny going into Goon's house this morning as a red-
headed messenger-boy-and coming out just myself, and
nobody spotting me ! Come-on let's go for a walk by
the river. It'll be cool there. I shall fall asleep in this
heat !'

As they went down the drive they met Mr. Goon
cycling up. They wondered which of the household he
was going to see. He stopped and got off his bike.

'You know that there telegraph-boy, that brought you
that telegram some time back ?' he said. 'Well, I happen
to know he's fake, see ? There's no telegraph-boy like
that. And I'm making strict inquiries into the matter, I
am-yes and into fake telegrams too, see ? And I warn
you all, if you hob-nob with red-heads, you'll get into Serious
Trouble. Very Serious Trouble'.

'You do frighten me,' said Fatty, making his eyes go
big.

'And I'll have None of your Sauce !' said Mr. Goon
majestically. 'I know more than what you think, and I advise
you all to be careful. Call that dog orf !'

'Come here, Buster,' said Fatty, in such a mild voice that Buster took no notice at all. He went on prancing round Mr. Goon's ankles.

'I said, call him *orf* !' repeated Mr. Goon, doing little prances too, to avoid sudden rushes by Buster.

'Come here, Buster.' said Fatty again, in an extremely polite voice. Buster ignored him completely.

'That's not calling him orf !' shouted Mr. Goon, beginning to lose his temper. 'Yell at him, go on ! Nuisance of a dog !'

Fatty winked at the others, and with one accord they all opened their mouths and yelled at the top of their voices. 'COME HERE, BUSTER !'

Mr. Goon jumped violently at the noise. He glared. Buster also jumped. He went to Fatty.

'Not pleased even now, Mr. Goon ?' said Fatty sweetly. 'Oh dear-there's no pleasing you at all, I'm afraid. Wait a minute—I believe I've got a really good clue to hand you—ah, here it is!'

He took out a match-box and gave it to the policeman. Mr. Goon opened it supiciously. It was a trick match-box, and, as Mr. Goon opened it, he released a powerful spring inside which sprang up and shot the match-box high in the air. Mr. Goon got quite a shock.

He went purple, and his eyes bulged.

'So sorry, so sorry,' said Fatty hastily. 'It must have been the wrong match-box. Wait a bit-I've got another....?

If Buster had not been there with his ready teeth Mr. Goon might quite well have boxed Fatty's ears. He looked ready to burst. Fearing that he might say something he ought not to, poor Mr. Goon hurriedly mounted his bicycle and rode up the drive, breathing so heavily that he could be heard all the way to the kitchen-door.

'He's gone to talk to Mrs. Moon again,' said Pip. 'I expect they'll come to blows! Let's get on. Oh, Fatty, I thought I should burst when that trick match-box went up in the air. Goon's face !'

They strolled down the lane to the river. It was pleasant there, for a breeze blew across the water. The children found a sunny place beside a bigbush and lay down lazily. A swan came swimming by, and two moor-hens chugged across the water, their heads bobbing like clock-work.

'Let's forget all about the Mystery for a bit.' said Daisy. 'It's so nice here. I keep on thinking and thinking about those letters, and who could be writing them— but the more I think the less I know'.

'Same here,' said Pip. 'So many Suspects-and not one of them could apparently have Done the Deed. A most mysterious mystery'.

'One that even the great detective, Mr. Frederick Sherlock Holmes Trotteville can't solve either !' said Larry.

'Correct !' said Fatty, with a sigh. I almost—but not quite—give it up !'

Larry's hat blew away and he got up to go and get it. 'Blow !' he said. 'There's old Clear-Orf again—cycling over the field-path. He's seen me too. Hope he doesn't come and make a row again. He'd like to eat you alive, Fatty, you're aggravating'.

'Sit down quickly, in case he hasn't seen you,' said Daisy. 'We don't want him here.'

Larry sat down. They all watched the blue water flowing smoothly by . The moor-hens came back again, and a fish jumped at a fly. A very early swallow dipped down to the water. It was all very peaceful indeed.

'I should think old Clear-Orf didn't see me after all.' said Larry. 'Thanks goodness. I think I'am going to sleep. There's something very soothing about the gurgling of the water—a lovely, peaceful afternoon.

Heavy breathing disturbed the peace, and clumsy footsteps came over the grass towards their bush. Mr. Goon appeared, his face a familiar purple. He carried a small sack in his hand, and looked extremely angry. He flung the tittle sack down fiercely.

'More Clues, I suppose !' he sneered. 'More of your silly, childish jokes ! White rats and match boxes ! Huh ! Gah ! What a set of chiildren ! And now these Clues— hidden nicely under a bush for me to find, I suppose ? What do you think I am ? A nitwit ?'

The children were astonished at this outburst, and Bets was really alarmed. Fatty put out a quick hand on Buster's collar, for the little Scottie had got his hackles up and was growling fiercely, showing all his teeth.

'What's up, Goon ? said Fatty, in a sharp, rather grown-up voice.

'You know as well as I do !' said the policeman. 'More Clues ! I suppose you'll tell me next that you don't know anything about that sack of Clues ! Gah !'

'What sack ? What clues ?' said Fatty, really puzzled. 'No—I really don't know what you're talking about,

Mr. Goon.'

'You don't know—ho no, you don't know !' said Mr. Goon, and he laughed a nasty laugh. 'You don't know anything about red wigs, either, I suppose ? Or writing rude letters to the Law ? Well, I know a lot ! Oho, don't I ? I'll teach you to lay clues about for me to find. Think I'm a real hignoramus, don't you.

'Shut up, Buster,' said Fatty, for Buster was now snarling very loudly indeed. 'Mr. Goon, please go. You're frightening little Bets, and I don't think I can hold Buster in much longer. I dont't know *what* you're talking about—and certainly I've never seen the sack before.'

Buster gave such a fearfully loud snarl that Mr. Goon thought it would be best to do as Fatty said and go. He went, leaving the little sack on the ground, and stepped heavily away looking as majestic as he could.

'Well, what an unpleasant fellow,' said Fatty, slipping his arm round Bets, who was in tears. 'Don't bother about him, Bets. We know the blustering, roaring old fellow by now. You need never he scared of *him* !'

'I don't like p-p-people to shout like that,' sobbed Bets. 'And oh Fatty, he said about your red wig! Has he found it?'

'I wondered about that to,' said Fatty. 'We'll look when we go back. I left it in the summer house, didn't I ? Wish I hadn't now.'

'What's this sack of clues that old Clear-Orf kept yammering about ?' said Larry. He pulled it towards him. 'Some old collection of rubbish some tramp had left behind him under a bush, I suppose—and Mr. Goon found it and thought it was some more of your false clues, Fatty, planted for him to find.'

Larry undid the neck of the little sack. It was not much bigger than a three-pound flour bag. Inside, half-wrapped in brown paper, were some curious things.

There was a small school dictionary—and when he saw it Pip sat up in surprise. 'Golly ! That's my dicky. I do declare !' he said. The one I lost last hols. Isn't it, Bets ? Gracious, how did it get into this sack ?'

This made every one sit up and take notice at once. Fatty reached out his arm and took the sack. He ran his fingers quickly throgh the dictionary, and noted that several words were underlined. One of them was 'thief'. Another was 'fruit'. Fatty found others, all underlined.

Pip's name was in the front of the dictionary. There was no doubt at all but that it was his lost book. Fatty put his hand into the sack to see what else there was there.

He drew out—an alphabet book. 'A is for Apple, so rosy and red !' he chanted, 'B is for Baby who's just off to bed.' My goodness, no wonder old Clear-Orf thought we'd planted these things for him—a dictionary—and an alphabet book. Most peculiar !'

The next thing was a child's copy-book with some of the pages filled in, not very neatly. Larry laughed.

'This is some village kid's little treasure-store, I should think,'he said. 'Though goodness knows how the kid got hold of Pip's dictionary.'

Fatty dipped his hand in again. His eyes were suddenly very bright indeed. He pulled out an old bus time-table. He looked at it and then flipped it. It fell

Fatty dipped his hand in again

open at one much-thumbed page—and on that page there was a mark.

'Do you know what is marked ?' said Fatty. 'The 10.15 bus to Sheepsale ! What do you think of that ?'

The others stared at him. They were all very puzzled now. Fatty spoke excitedly.

'These are *real* Clues ! Don't you understand, you donkeys ? Goon thought they were silly, false ones put there by us to deceive him—but they're *real* ones, ones that may help us to put our hand on the letter-writer this very day.'

Now it was the turn of the others to get excited. 'Oooh,' said Bets. 'How silly of Mr. Goon to give them all to *us*.'

Fatty put his hand in once again and drew out a little, torn scrap of paper with some untidy writing on it. There were only two or three words to be made out. One was 'spoonful'. another was 'stir,' and another was 'oven'. Fatty read them and nodded. He was evidently very pleased indeed with this find.

'Poor old Goon !' he said. 'He makes the one glorious find in this Mystery—and throws it down at our feet. Won't he kick himself when he knows? What a bit of luck, oh what a bit of luck !'

THE other four tried in vain to make Fatty tell them more. But he wouldn't. 'You can look at all these clues as much as you like,' he said, 'and if you use your brains they will tell you exactly what they tell me. Exactly. I could tell you everything in two minutes—but I do really think you should try to find out what I have found out.'

'But that silly alphabet book !' said Daisy. 'It doesn't tell me a thing !'

'And all that time-table tells me is that there's a bus to Sheepsale at 10.15, and it's the bus the letter-writer probably took—but it doesn't tell me anything else,' said Pip. 'As to my dictonary—well that beats me !'

'Come on—let's get back home,' said Fatty. 'I've got to think this all out. It's not a scrap of good going to Goon about it. He won't believe a word. In fact I think he's got it firmly in his head that I'm mixed up in all this letter-writing. I'm sure he thinks I wrote the letter to him !'

'Well—who are we going to, then ? asked Bets. 'Inspector Jenks? I'd like that !'

'I thought perhaps we'd better tell your mother first,' said Fatty. 'I don't somehow feel as if I want to bring Inspector Jenks down here for an affair like this-and go right over Goon's head with the clues that Goon himself presented us with. Doesn't seem quite fair somehow'.

'It seems quite fair to *me* !' said Bets, who disliked

Mr. Goon more than any of the others did. 'Oh, Fatty—tell us all you know from these clues, do, do, do !'

'Now, Bets, if you like to think hard and study these clues, you would know as much as I do,' said Fatty. 'Come on—let's go home and on the way you can all think hard and if nobody can find out what these clues mean, or who they're pointing to, then I'll tell you myself. But give your brains a chance, do!'

In silence except for Buster's occasional yaps at a stray cat, they went home to Pip's. When they got into the drive they saw a big black car there.

'Whose is that ?' said Bets, in wonder.

'And there's Mr. Goon's bike,' said Daisy, pointing to where it stood by the front door. 'He's here too.'

Mrs. Hilton suddenly opened the front door and stood there, waiting for them, looking pale and worried.

'Come in this way,' she said. 'I'm glad you've come. Mr. Goon is here—saying most peculiar things—and he's got Inspector Jenks over too !'

'Oh! Is *he* here ?' cried Bets in delight, and rushed into the drawing-room. The big Inspector sat there, his eyes twinkling as he saw Bets. He was very fond of her.

She flung herself on him. 'I haven't seen you since the Christmas holidays ! You're bigger than ever ! Oh—there's Mr. Goon !'

So there was, sitting upright in a corner, looking curiously pleased with himself.

The other four came in more quietly, and shook hands with the big Inspector. They knew him well, for he had come to their help very often, when they were solving other problems. Buster capered round his ankles in delight, awaiting for the pat he knew would come.

Mrs.Hilton waited till the greetings were over, and then spoke in a worried voice.

'Children! Mr. Goon brought Inspector Jenks over here to-day, when he was visiting Peterswood, because he had a serious complaint to make of your behaviour, especially one of you, and he thought that it would be a good thing if the Inspector reprimanded you himself. But I cannot imagine what you have been doing-unless you have been interfering in this anonymous letter business—and I said you were not to.'

Nobody said anything. Fatty looked politely and inquiringly at the Inspector.

'Suppose you hold forth, Goon,' said the Inspector, in his pleasant, courteous voice. 'You have quite a lot to say, I believe.'

'Well, sir,' began Mr. Goon, in a righteous sort of voice, 'I know your opinion of these here children has always been high—but I've always known more of them than you have, if you'll pardon me saying so, sir—and they've bin getting above themselves, sir-meddling in things that don't concern them, and hindering me in my business, sir—and one of them—this here boy by name of Frederick Trotteville, sir, I regret to inform you that he has meddled in this anonmous writing, and sent me a most rude and incivil letter, sir—and what's more he goes about pretending to be what he's not, sir—and deceiving me proper-like,....'

'Exactly what do you mean by that, Goon ? asked the Inspector mildly. 'Going about pretending to be what he's not ?'

'Well, sir, he's a whole lot of red-headed boys, sir,' said Mr. Goon, to the great mystification of the Inspector and Mrs. Hilton. 'Took me in proper he did. First he was a red-headed telegraph-boy, sir—then he was a butcher-boy—and a messenger-boy, sir—tearing round on his bike, a public danger, sir, and a nuisance. But as soon as I found the red wig, sir......'

'Who told you where it was ?' asked Fatty.

'Mrs. Moon showed me,' said Mr. Goon. 'Yes, and she told me, too, all the things you've been saying about me, Master Frederick—you and the others—and how she overheard you planning to write that there cheeky letter to me !'

'Really ?' said Fatty his eys gleaming curiously. 'Perhaps she told you also, who is the writer of those other anonymous letters ?'

'Well, no, she didn't,' admitted Mr. Goon. 'Unless it was some one she's Got Her Eye On. But she wasn't mentioning any names just yet.'

'Frederick, this is all very disturbing,' said Mrs. Hilton., 'I cannot imagine what you have been doing ! And surely, surely you did not write that letter to Mr. Goon !'

'No, Mrs. Hilton, of course I didn't,' said Fatty. 'As for the disguises—well, I mean to be a famous detective when I grow up—and I'm just practising, that's all. I *have* been looking into the mystery of the anonymous letter-writing—and by great good luck I've had a whole lot of clues thrust upon me. As a matter of fact we were going to tell you the whole thing as soon as we got back.'

'Ho yes !' said Mr. Goon disbelievingly.

'That will do, Goon,' said the Inspector. 'What are these clues, Frederick, that you've had thrust upon you?'

Fatty went into the hall and came back with the little sack. He placed it on the table. Mr. Goon stared at it and his eyes bulged.

'Those clues!' he said, scornfully. 'Those clues you planted for me to find! Ho! Copybooks and alphabet books! White rats and match-boxes that jump! Clothing pegs and doll's hats!'

The Inspector looked most astonished at this long list of things. Fatty looked a little uncomfortable.

'Just my little joke,' he murmured.

'Well, your little jokes have landed you into Serious Trouble,' said Mr. Goon. 'Just like I said they would. It was lucky the Inspector was in Peterswood to-day. Soon as I told him about everything, along he came.'

'Very kind of him,' said Fatty. 'In fact, as far as we are concerned, he has come at exactly the right moment. We were just discussing whether or not we should telephone him and ask him to come over. Now he's here!'

'And what did you want to see me about?' asked the Inspector.

'About this anonymous letter-writing business, sir,' said Fatty. You see, we couldn't let a mystery like that happen under our very noses, so to speak, without going into it a bit. And we were all sorry for Gladys.'

'Quite so,' said the Inspector. 'Another case for the Five Find-outers-and Dog!'

'Yes, sir,' said Fatty. 'A very difficult affair too, sir, We got on a lot of wrong trails.'

'We found out that the letter-writer caught the 10.15 bus to Sheepsale,' said Bets. 'And we went on it on Monday, to see who the passengers were. but nobody posted a letter there!'

'Except Master Frederick!' shot out Mr. Goon. 'There—I told you Mr. Goon would put you down on his List of Suspects if he saw you posting that letter!' said Bets.

'I rather hoped he would!' said Fatty, with a grin. Mr. Goon scowled. This interview wasn't coming off quite as he had hoped it would. That wretched boy, Fatty! He always seemed to get away with anything. And the Inspector didn't seem to be taking the matter very seriously, either. It was too bad.

'I expect Mr. Goon has told you about the bus to Sheepsale, though Sir, and how, the letters were always posted there by the 11.45 post,' said Fatty. 'And how nobody posted any that day—except me !—and I expect, like us, he made inquiries to see if any of the regular bus passengers failed to go on the bus that day for some reason or other-and got his Suspects narrowed down to Old Nosey, Miss Tittle, and Mrs. Moon'.

'Yes. He did tell me,' said the Inspector. 'And I think, if I may say so, that it was pretty smart work on the part of you children to work all that out !'

This was too much for Mr. Goon. 'Smart work! Interfering with the Law, that's what I call it,' he said. I suppose he'll tell you next that he knows who that letter-writer is!'

'Yes. I was going to come to that,' said Fatty quietly. 'I *do* know who the letter-writer is !'

Every one gaped at Fatty. Even the Inspector sat up

straight at once. As for Goon, his mouth fell open and he goggled at Fatty in disbelief.

'Who is it ?' he said.

'Mrs. Hilton—may I ring the bell ?' said Fatty. She nodded. He went over to the wall and rang the bell hard. Every one waited.

21   WELL DONE, FATTY !

THE bell sounded loudly. The door opened in the kitchen and footsteps came up the hall. Mrs. Moon appeared in the drawing-room. She looked surprised and rather scared when she saw so many people sitting quietly there.

'Did you ring, Madam?' she asked, and her voice shook a little.

'I rang.' said Fatty. He turned to the Inspector. 'This is the anonymous letter-writer,' he said. 'Mrs. Moon!'

Mrs. Hilton gasped. Mr. Goon snorted loudly. All the children drew in their breath sharply. Only the Inspector seemed unperturbed.

Mrs. Moon went pale. She stared at Fatty. 'What do you mean ?' she said fiercely. 'How dare you say things like that to a respectable law—abiding woman ?'

'Hardly law-abiding, Mrs.Moon,' said the Inspector's stern voice. 'It is against the law to send spiteful and untrue letters through the post anonymously. But Frederick—please explain. I have enough faith in your intelligence to know that you are making no mistake, if I may say so—but I want to know all about it.'

Mrs. Moon began to cry. 'Sit down and keep quiet,' commanded Inspector Jenks.

'I won't be treated like this, I won't !' wailed Mrs. Moon. An innocent woman like me! Why, I've even had one of them awful letters meself !'

'Yes-you nearly took me in over that' said Fatty. 'I thought that ruled you out-but it was just a bit of artfulness on your part. I see that now.'

'You bad, wicked boy!' moaned Mrs. Moon.

'Silence !' said the Inspector, in such a fierce voice that Bets jumped. 'Speak when you're spoken to, Mrs. Moon, and not unless. If you are innocent you will be given plenty of chance to prove it. We will hear what you have to say when Master Frederick has told his story. Frederick, begin.'

Fatty began, and the other childeren leaned forward, knowing most of the story well, but longing to hear what the end of it was. Only Fatty knew that.

'Well, sir, you know already that we worked out that as the letters were posted in Sheepsale each Monday to catch the 11.45 post there, that it was probable the guilty person was some one who took the 10.15 bus from Peterswood to Sheepsale.' said Fatty.

'Quite so.' said the Inspector.

'Well, we found that none of the bus-passengers last Monday could be the letter-writer,' said Fatty, 'and certainly none of them posted a letter. So then we decided to find out if any regular Monday passenger was *not* on the bus that Monday, and make inquiries about them. And as you know, we found that three regular passengers didn't travel that day—Miss Tittle, Old Nosey, and Mrs. Moon.'

'Mr. Goon also worked on the same lines,' said the Inspector. A sound from Goon made every one look up.

'How did you get to see them letters, and see the post-mark ?' demanded Mr. Goon. That's what I want to know.'

'Oh, that's not an important detail,' said Fatty, anxious not to give away Gladys' part in that affair. 'Well, to continue, sir—we found out next that another letter had been sent that Monday— but not from Sheepsale—it had been delivered by hand. So that definitely pointed to somebody in Peterswood, and possibly one of our three Suspects— Old Nosey, Miss Tittle, or Mrs. Moon.'

'Quite.' said the Inspector, deeply interested. I must say that your powers of deduction are good, Frederick.'

'Well, the letter was delivered very early in the morning,' said Fatty, 'so I had to find out which of the three Suspects was up early that Tuesday. And I found that all of them were !'

'Very puzzling,' said the Inspector. 'I don't think Mr. Goon got quite as far as that, did you, Mr. Goon ? Go on, Frederick.'

'That rather shook me,' said Fatty, 'and the only thing I could think of next was getting specimens of the handwriting of each of the three—to compare with the printed letters, you see.'

'A good idea,' said Inspector Jenks, 'but surely a little difficult ?'

'Not very,' said Fatty modestly. 'You see, I put on a disguise—a red-headed delivery-boy I was.' There was a snort from Mr. Goon at this. 'And,' went on Fatty, 'I just delivered parcels to all three, and got them to sign receipts in capital letters—so that I could compare them with the capital letters in the anonymous notes!'

'Most ingenious, if I may say so,' said the Inspector. He turned to Mr. Goon, whose eyes were bulging at hearing about all this detective work on Fatty's part. 'I am sure you agree with me ?' said the Inspector. Mr. Goon did not agree with him at all, but couldn't very well say so.

'Well, I found that Nosey couldn't write at all,' said Fatty. 'So that ruled him out. Then I saw that Miss Tittle's printing, very small and neat and beautiful, wasn't anything at all like the printing of the letters in the anonymous notes-and that rather ruled *her* out too-and to my surprise Mrs.Moon's printing was such a mixture of big and small letters that I couldn't think she could be the culprit either.'

'And I'm not!' said Mrs. Moon, rocking herself to and fro. 'No, I'm not.'

'Here's a specimen of her writing—or rather, printing sir,' said Fatty, opening his notebook and showing the Insector Mrs. Moon's curious printing, big and small letters mixed. 'When I asked her about it, she gave me to understand that she couldn't help it—it appeared to me, sir, that she was muddled in her mind as to which were big and which were small letters.'

'Quite,' said Inspector Jenks. So you ruled her out too, as the messages and the addresses on the anonymous letters were apparently printed quite correctly in capitals, with no small letters at all ?'

'Yes, sir,' said Fatty.'And I almost gave up the case. Couldn't see any light anywhere—and hadn't got any real clues, either. I didn't think at the time, either, that Mrs. Moon would write an anonymous letter to herself—though I *should* have thought of that, of course. . . .'

'And what about that letter to *me* ?'said Mr.Goon, suddenly. 'That was you, wasn't it, Master Frederick ? Come on, you own up now—that was you, calling me a meddler and a muddler and cheeking me like you always do !'

'No—I certainly didn't write you that letter,' said Fatty. And I think if you compare it with the others, Mr. Goon, you'll see it's just like them.'

'Well, Frederick—how did you come to know in the end that it *was* Mrs. Moon and nobody else ?' inquired the Inspector.

'I tell you it wasn't, it wasn't,' moaned Mrs. Moon.

'That was a sheer bit of luck, sir,' said Fatty, modestly. 'Can't give myself any marks for that ! It was Mr. Goon who put me right on the track !'

'Gah !' said Mr. Goon disbelievingly.

'Yes—he suddenly gave us a whole sack of clues— that sack of things on the table !' said Fatty. 'And, as soon as I saw them I was able to piece things together and know who had written those disgusting, spiteful letters!'

The Inspector picked up the things one by one and looked at them with interest. 'Exactly what did these things tell you?' he said curiously.

'There's a dictionary, sir—with Pip's name in,' said Fatty. 'That told me that it probably came from this house and was used by somebody living here. Then I noticed that various words had been looked up for the spelling, and had been underlined—and every one of those words, sir, has been used in the anonymous letters !'

Mr. Goon's face went redder than ever. To think that boy had got all that out of the things in that sack !

'The next thing, sir, was the alphabet book,' said Fatty. 'And, as I daresay you've noticed, the alphabet letters in such a book are always in capitals. A is for Apple, and so on . So I guessed that book had been bought as a kind of reference book for capital letters, by somebody who wasn't quite sure of the difference in shape of big and small letters. The capital letter G, for instance, is quite different from the small letter g. Naturally the anonymous letter-writer didn't want to give away the fact that she hadn't had enough education to know the difference.'

'Well worked out, Frederick, well worked out,' said the Inspector, most interested. 'What about this ?' He held up the copybook.

'That's easy, sir,' said Fatty. 'Even Bets could read *that* clue now !'

'Yes, I can !' called Bets. 'That's a copybook Mrs. Moon must have bought to practise writing capital letters in. There's lots of capitals printed there in pencil.'

'I expect if you ask at the stationer's, Inspector, you'll find that Mrs. Moon did buy a copybook there some weeks ago !'

'Make inquiries, Goon,' said the Inspector. Goon hurriedly made a note in his notebook.

'The bus time-table was an easy clue,' said Fatty. 'I

guessed I'd find that 10.15 bus marked. And this bit of
torn paper, sir—used as a bookmark in the dictionary, I
should think—must have been torn from a recipe of some
sort. I knew that as soon as I read the words— 'spoonful'—'stir'—'oven'. I except you will find that they are in
Mrs. Moon's ordinary handwriting, and torn from her
kitchen recipe-book.'

'A most ingenious reading of rather peculiar clues !'
said the Inspector, looking really pleased. 'What a pity,
Mr. Goon you didn't take the trouble to look carefully
through the clues yourself, and deduct from them all
that Frederick has done.'

'Thought they was all false clues,' muttered Mr.
Goon. 'Made me angry, they did.'

'It's a mistake to let anger cloud your thinking, Goon.'
said the Inspector. 'If you had only examined these clues
carefully, you might have arrived at the same conclu-
sions as Frederick here—but again, you might not !'

It was apparent that the Inspector believed that Goon
would certainly not have made such good use of the
clues as Fatty had !

Mrs. Moon suddenly threw her apron over her head
and wailed loudly. She rocked to and fro again, and Bets
watched her in dismay. She didn't like people who
shouted and howled.

'You're all against me, you are !' wailed Mrs. Moon.
'Not a friend have I got in the world ! You're all against
me !'

'You have only yourself to blame, my good
woman,' said Inspector Jenks sharply.' 'You yourself are

apparently filled with spite against a great many people-and you cannot be surprised if you have no friends. I'm afraid you must come with me for further questioning. Mrs. Hilton, I fear that Mrs. Moon will not be returning to you.'

'I don't want her,' said Mrs. Hilton, with a shudder. 'A cruel, underhand, spiteful woman like that in my house ! No, never. Poor Gladys. I'll fetch her back at once. I'm horrified and disgusted, Mrs. Moon. You have caused a great deal of pain and grief to many people, and I hope you will be well punished'.

'You don't mind us having investigated the case now, Mother, do you ? said Pip, thinking this was a good opportunity to get his mother to agree.

'Well—I didn't want you mixed up in such an un-pleasant business,' said Mrs. Hilton. 'And I must say that I thought Mr. Goon could manage it himself. But I do think you worked out things very cleverly—espe-cially Fatty, of course.'

'Oh, all the Find-Outers did their bit,' said Fatty loy-ally. 'I couldn't have done without them. And,'he said, with a glance at Mr. Goon, 'we did have a lot of fun at times-didn't we, Pip ?'

'We did !' said all the others, and grinned at poor Mr. Goon, who did one of his snorts, and scowled heavily at them.

The Inspector got up. 'Get your outdoor things, Mrs. Moon,' he said. 'You must come with me. Goon, I want you too. But perhaps, when I have finished my work here, at about four o'clock this afternoon, Mrs. Hilton, the children could come over to Nutting, where I'm going then, and have tea with me in the big hotel there ? I feel I would like to have a little chat with the Five Find-Outers-and Dog--again !'

'Oooh !' said Bets, delighted.

'Woof,' said Buster, pleased.

'Oh thanks !' said the others.

Mrs. Moon went out, weeping. The Inspector shook hands with Mrs. Hilton and went out to his car. 'See you this afternoon !' he said, to the delighted children.

Mrs. Hilton went out to see that Mrs. Moon did what she was told. The children followed the Inspector to his black car. Mr. Goon was left behind in the drawing-room, looking gloomily at the carpet. He was alone with his thoughts.

No—he wasn't alone ! Buster was there too, regarding his old enemy with a bright eye. No one was there to say, 'Come here, Buster!' What a chance!

With a joyful yelp he flung himself at Mr. Goon's ankles, and pulled at his blue trousers. Mr. Goon rose up in alarm.

'Clear-orf!'

The children heard the shouting and laughed at the familiar words. 'Poor old Clear-Orf,' said Bets. 'Always in trouble. Fatty, go and rescue him'.

Fatty went. Mr. Goon came out, frowning, trying to see if his trouser-ankles had been torn. Buster struggled in Fatty's arms.

'Get in, Goon, whilst you're safe,' said the Inspector, opening the door of the car. 'Ah, here is Mrs. Moon. The other side, please, Mrs. Moon. Goodbye, children—

and thanks for your help once more. I must say I'm pleased with the Five Find-Outers and Dog !'

'Oh well—I suppose we ought to thank Mr. Goon for all those clues !' said Fatty. He winked at the others, and they all opened their mouths together at once and chanted :

'THANKS, MR. GOON !'

And what did Mr. Goon reply ? Exactly what you would expect.

'GAH!'

Also available in the Mystery Series

THE MYSTERY OF THE BURNT COTTAGE

This is the first of Enid Blyton's thrilling mystery books. Fatty, Larry, Daisy, Pip, Bets–and Buster the dog–turn detectives when a mysterious fire destroys a thatched cottage in their village. Calling themselves the 'Five Find-Outers and Dog' they set out to solve the mystery and discover the culprit. The final solution, however, surprises the Five Find-Outers almost as much as Mr. Goon, the village policeman. They can hardly wait for the next mystery to come along!

THE MYSTERY OF THE DISAPPEARING CAT

The second book in the popular Mystery series in which the Find-Outers–Larry, Fatty, Daisy, Pip, Bets and Buster the dog–turn detectives again to solve a very puzzling mystery.

A valuable Siamese cat is stolen from next door and suspicion falls on the children's friend, Luke the gardener's boy. How can they find the real thief and clear Luke of blame, especially with Mr. Goon the policeman interfering as usual ? The Find-Outers are plunged into the middle of a first class mystery with only the strangest of clues to work on.

THE MYSTERY OF THE SECRET ROOM

This is the third book in the Mystery series.

It is the Christmas holidays, and the Five are looking for mysteries. Then out of the blue Pip discovers a room, fully furnished, at the top of an empty house. Whose room is it ? What is it used for ? This is the problem that must be solved in *The Mystery of the Secret Room.* With the help of their friend Inspector Jenks, the Five Find-Outers eventually reach a solution in this most entertaining book.

THE MYSTERY OF THE MISSING NECKLACE

The fifth book of the popular Mystery series, in which Fatty, Larry, Daisy, Pip, Bets–and Buster the dog, all play their parts as Find-Outers.

There are a great many clever burglaries going on and it is suspected that members of the gang have their meeting place, somewhere in Peterswood. The children naturally determine to solve the mystery, and they tumble into other mysteries, too, in the process. Who is the old man on the seat ? Who is Number Three ? Where is the missing necklace ? For once Mr. Goon, the policeman, defeats Fatty one strange night at the Waxworks Hall ! But it all ends up most unexpectedly and amusingly with the children finally triumphant.

THE MYSTERY OF THE HIDDEN HOUSE

The sixth adventure in the popular Mystery series about Larry, Fatty, Daisy, Pip, Bets and Buster–the Five Find-Outers and Dog.

When P.C. Goon's nephew, Ern, comes to Peterswood full of ideas of detecting, the Find-Outers think up a first-class mystery, complete with clues, and send both Ern and Mr Goon off on a wild-goose chase to Christmas Hill. But Ern loses his way and suddenly stumbles into what the Find-Outers are sure is a real mystery. Once again they are on the trail of a really thirlling mystery, but Fatty's love of disguises lands both him and Ern in a very tricky situation.